Best Laid Plans

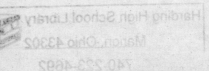

Best Laid Plans

Christine Hart

James Lorimer & Company Ltd.,
Publishers Toronto

James Lorimer & Company Ltd. acknowledges the support of the Canada Council for the Arts and the Ontario Arts Council for our publishing program. We acknowledge the financial support of the Government of Canada through the Book Publishing Industry Development Program (BPIDP) for our publishing activities. We acknowledge the Government of Ontario through the Ontario Media Development Corporation's Ontario Book Initiative.

Library and Archives Canada Cataloguing in Publication

Hart, Christine, 1978-
    Best laid plans / Christine Hart.
(Sidestreets)

ISBN 978-1-55277-447-2 (bound);—ISBN 978-1-55277-446-5 (pbk.)

        I. Title. II. Series: SideStreets

PS8615.A773B47 2009   jC813'.6   C2009-901679-6

James Lorimer & Company Ltd.,
Publishers
317 Adelaide Street West
Suite 1002
Toronto, Ontario
M5V 1P9
www.lorimer.ca

Distributed in the U.S. by:
Orca Book Publishers
P.O. Box 468
Custer, WA USA
98240-0468

Printed and bound in Canada.

*For Katie, who takes lemons and makes
lemon meringue pie.*

Thanks to my husband Jeff for all his encouragement and to the editors at James Lorimer and Company who recharged the battery on this novel.

Chapter 1

In the Okanagan Valley, apples aren't ripe and ready to pick until autumn. Each piece of fruit grows from a blossom and hangs on, waiting to be plucked off the branch. When an apple falls, never collected or eaten, it will soften in the grass. Starting with the bruise from the fall, the fruit will turn to mush, the seeds rotting inside. It happens slowly, but if you're not paying attention, the apple will be ruined, lost forever before you know it.

Looking down at a piece of fruit, half-ripe, half pulp, Robyn Earle wondered if she was becoming one of those apples. For over four years since the move from the tiny mountain town of Grand Forks to the Okanagan community of Coldstream, Robyn had been watching her parents struggle to grow fruit and maintain these trees. They all thought the apple business would come easily to them, but it didn't. Nothing did. And Robyn wanted out.

Robyn's family had inherited Hillside Orchard when her Grandma died; twenty acres of McIntosh, Spartan and Red Delicious apples. Before the orchard, most of her parents' money had come from the province. The government changed the name every few years — income assistance, employment assistance — but everyone just called it welfare. Mom had worked on and off as a cashier, waitress or cleaner, but a combination of chronic back pain and emotional "incidents" kept her at home a lot. Her dad looked for work once in a while, and sometimes he got a job, but it never lasted for long.

"I feel like I'm rotting," Robyn said. It was the end of an early September day, and Robyn was out at the far edge of the property with her fifteen-year-old sister Janeen, perched on a ladder and picking.

Janeen scoffed. "Give it a rest, Robyn. Jeez."

Robyn didn't like being dismissed but she didn't like to fight, either. She tried to think of a way to change the subject instead of arguing. "What are you and Caleb doing this weekend?"

"Why do you want to know?" asked Janeen through a puzzled frown.

"I don't know, I'm just making conversation," said Robyn, a little irritated.

"He's actually been getting on my nerves

lately. I'm thinking about breaking up with him," said Janeen.

"Oh," said Robyn.

"He's just, you know, pressuring me," Janeen mumbled as she looked down at her basket.

"Jan, you know you're way too young to be sleeping with someone!" Robyn blurted as her grip on her basket tightened.

"Shut up, *Mom*. Let's talk about something a little happier. When's the first senior house-wrecker? Or are you guys planning for a bush party?" Janeen said.

Robyn pulled her long hair into a ponytail. "I don't know; I'm not planning any parties. This year is going to be about getting into college for me. If I keep my grades up, maybe I can get into a university in Vancouver or out east somewhere. I could really do it if I can get a student loan." She was trying to sound optimistic, but her stomach twisted as she voiced a dream she knew far better than to get her hopes up for.

"Ha, Mom and Dad are never going to go for that. Maybe they'll let you go to college in town, but there's no way they're going to let you take out loans or move away," said Janeen.

"Why should they decide? Even if they don't let me go right away, they can't keep me here forever. Am I supposed to stay here and have kids so I can exploit them as apple pickers?"

"Well, they're not going to let you leave," Janeen said.

"Remember how I went on that trip to Vancouver, the one Hanna and her drama class?" Robyn asked.

"Yeah, you were making those ready-to-bake pies in the cafeteria for days before as a fund-raiser and you just about lost it after the apple batch," Janeen laughed.

"We were downtown, with these giant buildings all around us, and they were just so beautiful. I'd never seen anything like it. It was like another world. If I could conceive one of those towers myself, it would be the most amazing thing I'd ever do. That's the kind of art that lasts and makes a mark, you know?" Robyn said, looking past her sister at the horizon.

Janeen leaned on her bucket, speechless for a moment as she stared back at Robyn. "Wow, I had no idea you felt that strongly. But you know Dad ..." said Janeen quietly.

Chapter 2

The familiar bay window above the main doors at Lakeside Secondary seemed brighter Monday morning. To Robyn, the creamy stucco looked a little fresher, although she knew it couldn't possibly be any different. She felt a satisfying sense of confidence now that she was a senior. This was going to be her last year in this place.

As she walked towards the front doors, she scanned the grounds for familiar faces. Robyn's friends usually hung out by a bridge over a nearby creek, to keep their distance from the school. It wasn't worth it in the winter, but as long as the weather was good, hanging out with her friends outside was better than sitting inside alone. Her two best friends, Hanna and Becca, were at a granite picnic table near the bank, where they always were.

"Hey, Rob," Hanna yelled from her seat. "Get your ass over here!"

Robyn broke into a jog, excited to see her friends. It had been weeks since she had seen Hanna and Becca. While she had bided her time, buried in apples, Hanna and Becca went on glamorous family vacations.

"What classes are you in today? I've got Earth Science and Drama," said Hanna. She was one of the most outgoing friends Robyn had. She didn't get top marks in academic subjects, but Hanna could command a stage as though she belonged there.

"I'm in Art and CADD. It's kind of sad actually; these will probably be my favourite classes for the whole year and they'll be done before I know it," Robyn said.

"Oh my God, Robyn. You are such a geek," Becca said through a wide smile. "I doubt I'm going to miss any of my classes once this school sees the backside of me."

Robyn rolled her eyes.

"Rob, I love your dorky side," Hanna said as she stood up to collect her things.

"It's what makes you so fun to watch at parties," Becca added, playfully knocking her hip into Robyn's as they started back towards the school.

Robyn laughed at Becca. "*You're* the one that's fun to watch at parties. You *love* to give everyone a show!" Becca wasn't a good student or a budding superstar, but she was definitely a social butterfly — and very resourceful. She could scrounge enough change for fries and a pop, plan a party, start two rumours and still have time to flirt with one of her many crushes before a lunch hour was over.

"Ooo, I almost forgot … ladies, I have a beyond kick-ass plan for our first day," said Becca, pausing to be sure she had their undivided attention as they walked.

"Well, what?" said Hanna.

"After school, we'll all go get tattoos! It'll be freakin' amazing! We'll be like ink sisters! My brother's friend will do the work under the table, so we don't have to worry about the underage thing," she gushed.

"Seriously? That sounds awesome! I totally still want my dolphin," said Hanna.

"Rob, do you still want that ladybug?" said Becca. Robyn had loved ladybugs ever since her aunt Trish had told her she could make a wish when one landed on her.

"Yeah, but there's one little problem. Money. Specifically that I have none," said Robyn flatly. She always missed out on anything that cost more than five bucks.

"Maybe, between Hanna and me, we could cover yours too. This guy is just charging for ink 'cause he's doing it under the table. He needs to build his portfolio or whatever. We have to at least try," said Becca.

"Okay then. I'm game," said Robyn, knowing she could back out later if she had second thoughts.

"Nice! This is gonna be so amazing!" said Becca.

The bell rang just as they reached the doors. Robyn sprinted off, eager to get to class, her head swimming with the prospect of a tattoo. She barrelled down the hall, slowing just before she turned into the familiar art studio. She took in the impressionist and surrealist posters around the room as she searched for an open seat. The cute guy from last year's class, Nathan, sat in the second-to-last row by the window. She looked at him — she couldn't help it. And he looked back at her. And smiled. But no guy had ever "liked" her before, and she didn't see how this could be any different. She didn't want to get caught staring at him or embarrass herself trying to talk to him, so she took a seat in the front row by the disgustingly dirty sink.

"Good morning, creative geniuses. I hope the summer treated you all well. As you know, my expectations for senior students are considerably higher at this level, so if some of you are looking for an easy credit, I suggest you look elsewhere."

It actually gave Robyn a sense of satisfaction when Mrs. Campbell threatened lazy kids who didn't really care. She loved being there, spending her time listening to music and crafting intricate artwork on paper and canvas. Whatever she worked on, she wanted it to be better than good. She had to be sure each piece was excellent; the kids who didn't care were just wasting everyone's time.

After a lunch spent discussing the finer points of tattoo selection over one of her mom's standard processed cheese sandwiches and a pudding cup, Robyn was all raw nerves walking towards her afternoon class. Body art was the least of her worries. Now that she was old enough to take Computer-Aided Drafting and Design, or CADD, she finally had to put her dream of becoming an architect to a real-world test. The math and computer skills she needed already freaked her out. Math was hard, but living in a house without a computer left her at a distinct disadvantage compared to the other students.

Sitting in the cold basement computer lab, Robyn found herself intimidated by stark chalk diagrams on the blackboard and blueprints on the wall. Mr. Frank, the CADD teacher, paced at the front of the room, impatient as the last few stragglers found their seats.

"Good afternoon future draftspersons, construction trades enthusiasts and potential architects. Welcome to Computer-Aided Drafting and Design. For many of you, this class will be your first introduction to AutoCAD software and basic design principles," said Mr. Frank with none of Mrs. Campbell's smiling energy as he continued to pace back and forth in front of the blackboard.

"The assignments in this class are difficult and the pace of work is brisk. Although this isn't a provincially examinable subject, I expect high levels of commitment and performance on assignments and exams. If you succeed in this class, you may want to pursue similar training at a post-secondary level. If not, you may wish to drop this class before what you thought would be an easy pass turns out to be the 'D' that blocks your graduation," he said coldly.

Robyn's sweaty hand dropped her mechanical pencil and shot straight up. "If you're thinking about a career in architecture, would a university look at the grade in this class?" she asked shakily, betrayed by her nerves.

"I'm glad you're enthusiastic Miss …"

"Robyn Earle."

"I don't think I've had you in any of my classes before," said Mr. Frank, looking at her over the rim of his glasses. He hadn't met her before because she had never taken any of his metal shop, woodworking or automotive classes.

Mr. Frank picked his lecture up again and talked for the rest of the afternoon. By the end of the day, Robyn's mood hung low, weighted by the dread that she just wasn't smart enough. She sat on the lawn by the bus loading lane, worried and filled with self-doubt.

Hanna pulled up in the Saturn her parents had bought for her birthday the year before, with Becca bouncing excitedly in the front passenger seat.

"Hey, Robyn! Ready to go get inked?" Hanna called out through the open window.

"Oh yeah — that," said Robyn.

"Don't sound so excited! This is a fun thing that you *want* to do, remember?" said Becca.

"Seriously, don't worry about the money. I'm sure we'll get yours," said Hanna, anticipating her friend's next words.

Robyn looked down at the pavement. She put her books back in her bag and got into the car.

"Dangerous Designs is open until four o'clock on weekdays. We've got to wait until the place closes so that Kale — that's Mike's friend — doesn't get in trouble for doing our tattoos," Becca explained as Hanna drove.

Robyn frowned at the sketchy plan, but she was determined to get in on this rite of passage. She also prepared herself for the shop to be too crowded after hours or the tattoos to cost too much to include hers. Robyn had become a pro at anticipating and handling disappointment.

Dangerous Designs was actually a converted two-bedroom house on a rundown lot, now out of place with a light industrial area on one side, apartment buildings and retail storefronts on the other.

They arrived to find a half-dozen bulky thirty-something men pacing around the living room turned waiting room. From their large steel hoop earrings, shaved hairstyles and various jewellery-brand T-shirts, Robyn guessed that one or more were owners of the shop. Robyn and Hanna followed Becca's lead, slipping past the group into a pair of folding chairs behind the photo mosaic coffee table.

Hanna pretended to be deeply interested in the contents of her backpack while Robyn attempted her best doe-eyed look, scanning the wall of photos and paying particular attention to the section on tongue piercings.

"Hey, little girls … are you looking for something?" sneered a burly, amply pierced man with a long goatee.

"Don't worry about it; they're with me. That's Mike's little sister," said Kale suddenly from behind the front counter. Robyn shifted uneasily as her chair creaked in complaint.

"Um, we're here to uh, just look around," Becca said to Kale. Normally Becca was the picture of confidence, but she was out of her element here and none of them were sure how discreet they needed to be. Fortunately, the men in the waiting room soon decided it was time to leave.

"Can we take a look at your books so we can get an idea on price?" asked Becca after the last man was out the door. "We're not sure we can cover what we all had in mind. You're just charging for ink, right?" she asked.

"I'm sure we can work something out," Kale said calmly. Robyn was glad he didn't seem concerned about getting caught.

The girls flipped through the large binders of artwork and soon each of them had a design picked out. Becca explained that she and Hanna would go first, each paying for their own, and then it would be Robyn's turn if they had enough left between them to cover what she wanted.

It felt like hours before he finished Hanna and Becca's tattoos. Robyn kept flipping through the plastic-coated binder pages long after she decided on a quarter-sized ladybug. Intense boredom and nervousness gripped her as she worried that she might see something to make her change her mind.

She paced around the room, looking out the window at the row of shops and offices down the street. She remembered hearing about the youth employment centre with the big purple sign. Why wasn't she over there researching schools or trying to get a job?

Finally, Kale negotiated the price for the first two tattoos and there was enough money left for one more. He escorted Robyn to one of the back rooms, manoeuvred what looked like an old dentist's chair, and asked her to sit on it sideways with her back to him. Trying to slow the speed of her thoughts and her racing heartbeat, she examined the floor-to-ceiling bamboo blinds covering sliding glass doors several feet away.

Robyn sat rigid with tension as Kale folded her jeans down farther than she already had, swabbed her hip with cold alcohol and proceeded to shave her bare skin. He dried her off and carefully placed the stencil on her hip. The wet cloth he used to transfer the stencil was sopping and water dripped down, soaking into her pants. By the time he mixed his ink and started the gun Robyn had relaxed a bit. Like the chair, the sound of the tattooing gun reminded her of a dentist's office.

"I'm going to do the outline first. That's the thickest line and it hurts the most, so once you get through that part, the worst is over," Kale said and smiled for the first time.

The presence of his hands, one stretching her skin and bracing, the other holding the gun, was followed quickly by a brief prick. A few more light prickling touches and Robyn felt fresh excitement; this wasn't bad at all.

Then a deep, dull pain like she had never felt before drilled into her hip. She was sure something was wrong, but she kept quiet so Kale could concentrate. Again, an incredible hot pain seared through her. It felt like a molten, blunt blade was being pushed hard into her hip. Over and over again, the needle went in, relieved only by Kale wiping ink and blood off Robyn's skin with a wet paper towel. Her skin was soon raw and throbbing. *How horrible will a half-done tattoo look, if I just get up and run out of here?* she thought. *Can I get it finished another day? Will he yell at me?* She squeezed her eyes together tighter. *No, I can handle this. I have to. I've got to sit still and keep quiet. It has to end sometime.*

"How are you doing over there?" Kale must not have expected a response, because he kept talking. "The outline is about three-quarters done, so not too much longer," he said and set his gun down for a moment. Robyn sensed the heat of blush in her cheeks, embarrassed that he must be able to tell she was having real trouble with the pain. If she wanted out, now was the time to speak up, before he gripped her hip again.

"I'm sorry. I can't do this," she blurted. "I can't stay here anymore. I know it's not done, but I'm sorry," she said, rushing through every thought and emotion in her head.

"It's really not going to be much longer if you can just hang on," he said.

"I can't. I can't do it. Can you please bandage it up?" she pleaded.

"I'm not going to be able to do this again. I told Becca this was a one-time deal and if you don't let me finish, you're stuck with half a tattoo," he said curtly.

"I understand," said Robyn, feeling a deep nausea and an urgent need to pee. Kale dried her hip, applied some balm and bandaged her up.

Robyn hung her head as she followed Kale out front where he explained to Hanna and Becca why there wasn't much extra charge. Her friends looked disappointed, but no one said a word.

Chapter 3

After a quiet, tense car ride, Robyn arrived home to find the front screen door dismantled on the porch. Her dad was kneeling beside the door with a hammer in one hand, poking around in a jar of loose screws with other. She paused and waited for him to look up, but he was completely unaware of her presence.

"Why exactly is the screen door off its hinges?" she said, knowing fully that she was looking at another one of her father's repair projects.

"Never you mind; I've got it under control. Go eat your dinner," her dad grumped.

"Mom … Dad's wrecking the door!" she called ahead bravely as she walked past.

"Don't be such a wiseass!" said her dad with a snap.

Robyn knew he was going to have a lot of

trouble with that door. He had tried to fix the tool shed, tattered apple baskets, broken ladders, and even the roof last year. His attempts to fix things usually ended in a crappy job, the problem made worse and left hanging, or marginally improved by one of his buddies coming to "help out" with a six-pack. But Robyn hoped his project — and the inevitable argument with her mom — would keep them from noticing the crinkling bandage poking out over her jeans.

As she watched from the living-room window, her dad must have lost patience with some tool or fastener because he suddenly got up, walked over to his truck and drove off.

It was long after dark by the time her dad got home again. Robyn and her mom were both sitting in the living room, watching TV and ignoring each other.

"Will, where the hell were you all night? I was starting to get worried," her mom asked.

"I was just down at the pub. I'm entitled to a break now and then," he said.

"Well I'm glad one of us got to take a break tonight," she said through the cigarette she was about to light.

"We got any beer in the fridge?" he asked walking straight past her.

"No, we're way too short on cash this month."

Robyn thought about leaving, but instead she stayed and watched, hugging her knees.

"Aren't you going to finish up with the screen

door?" her mom grumbled.

"Not tonight, my show's on soon," he said.

Robyn's mom sank down into the couch, fuming. Robyn suspected she was mad because of the money her dad had just spent. Whether he drank at the pub or brought beer home, the cost of liquor was always a sore point. On a night like this, if she got in the right mood, she would start complaining to whoever would listen about how many wives had it better than she did.

As the inevitable argument began, Robyn decided to leave after all. She went up to Janeen's room to talk to someone who wouldn't depress her. She found her sister reading a note that had obviously been unfolded and refolded many times.

"Whatcha doin'?" Robyn teased as she sat heavily on Janeen's bed.

"Trying to read; can't you tell?" Janeen snapped.

"Feel like talking about it?" asked Robyn sympathetically. Unlike her mother she thought Janeen would be taking a firm stand with Caleb, who probably wrote the note.

"No, but you can help me take my mind off it," said Janeen.

"Actually, I have just the thing. Guess what moronic, ridiculously stupid move your big sis just pulled." Robyn unbuttoned her jeans and peeled back her waistband enough to show off her bandage.

"You got inked!" shrieked Janeen.

"Shhhhh! Shut up, or Mom and Dad will hear you!" Robyn said, taking a deep breath to tell the worst of it. "It's not just that I got a tattoo. It's only half-done. It hurt so bad that I had to get him to stop. I practically ran out of there," said Robyn.

Janeen put the note on her milk crate nightstand. "Oh my God, that's so harsh. Are you okay? Do you need anything?"

"Nah, I just wanted to talk to someone. Mom and Dad are downstairs fighting," said Robyn.

"What else is new? They've always had vicious timing for fights. Let me know if there's anything I can do," said Janeen as she gave Robyn a tight squeeze. Robyn winced as her hip twisted. She said goodnight and walked down the hall to her own room.

Robyn rolled back and forth in bed, staring at the ceiling at her beloved poster of Pete Wentz and her dad's wrinkled old Metallica poster. What was she going to do with half a tattoo? And why did her dad have to be such a loser? Couldn't he try harder, accept responsibility and get his life together? If he hadn't done it by now, was he too old to change? She fell into a restless sleep, but only after the frustrated, angry chatter in her head wore her out.

The weekend came quickly. Robyn had somewhat successfully put the tattoo out of her mind so she could focus on chores and homework. First thing Saturday morning, Robyn, her mom,

Janeen and their only regular picker, Bruce, all headed into the trees after breakfast. Her dad had left without explanation shortly after sunrise. Her mom had a big flat trolley for getting buckets and baskets up and down the rows. Everybody wore large straw hats. Fall days were getting colder, but the Okanagan sun could still blast out a sunburn on a clear day.

During peak picking, most orchards had several teams working to cover more area quickly. But this year it was just the four of them, without her dad. Each of them grabbed a basket and a ladder off the trolley.

"We're not getting any other help?" Janeen asked bluntly.

"We'll see, Sweetie. Your dad'll help too as soon as he's finished his errands," their mom answered with a forced pleasant tone, hiding her usual bitterness for Bruce's benefit.

"Yeah, well, I could be at the mall with Lisa today. I don't think it's exactly fair for Rob and I to get stuck with all the work this year," said Janeen.

"I know. We'll figure out something better soon, but today, we've all got to pitch in," she answered. She sounded drained before the work had even begun.

"Um, Valerie? Can I have a word aside for a minute?" Bruce asked their mom cautiously. Bruce was usually pretty quiet and he only spoke to Dad most of the time.

He and their mom walked a couple of rows over and started speaking in hushed voices. Robyn strained to hear.

"I wouldn't normally make trouble about money, but Will's a week late on my wages already and …" he continued, inaudible to Robyn. She didn't need to hear any more to know what mood her mom would be in afterwards.

Not long before dinner, her dad came home smelling powerfully of cigarettes and whisky.

"Will, what the hell have you been up to all day? What are you thinking, drinking with your friends while your kids take care of this orchard?" their mother demanded.

He pulled a small roll of twenties out of his back pocket. Robyn sucked in a deep breath, wondering what was missing from their house that would now be in some pawn shop in town. Sometimes he rode his bike around, collecting bottles in a makeshift milk crate basket so he could return them for the refund. But he obviously hadn't been riding a bike all day and bottles wouldn't have earned him that much. Robyn's dream of their family owning a computer drifted farther away each time he sold something.

"I was out making money. You said we were a little short this month. You're not gonna argue with extra cash are you?" he asked.

Janeen and Robyn finished setting the table while their mom brought out a small chicken, vegetables, dinner rolls, gravy and mashed potatoes.

"We need you here, earning money instead of selling the last few things we own. If we don't pull it together this fall, we're going to be short on more than a few orders. Bruce asked about his wages today, which are late already," said her mom.

"Don't tell me how to run my orchard," he said sharply.

"This is *my* parents' orchard. And maybe *I* should be running it. God knows you've screwed it up enough times," she snapped back.

"I don't need this again." He stood up and pulled the money back out of his pocket. Counting out what he owed, he set a small pile of bills next to his wife's plate.

Then he walked away without saying anything else. Robyn, Janeen and their mom finished the meal in silence.

Chapter 4

The sun had barely set when Uncle Ted's station wagon rolled onto the gravel drive and up to the house. Uncle Ted and Aunt Sue stretched their tired bodies as they got out of the car.

Robyn felt guilty about it, but wondered if this meant that her aunt and uncle would be staying with them. And if so, for how long? Uncle Ted walked over to Robyn's dad and wrapped his younger brother in a bear hug, and then he threw his arms around Robyn and the pungent smell of body odour overpowered her. Uncle Ted's dingy, stained T-shirt and unshaven jaw suggested he'd been travelling for hours.

"I hope we're not imposing," he said. "Do you have room?"

Her mom appeared on the porch, tea towel in hand, listening, with Janeen close behind.

"Don't be silly; we'll make room. Right girls?" her dad said with a fresh smile, not making eye contact with either daughter.

Aunt Sue followed behind Ted. Her vibrant yellow perm was barely dulled by the dusk light, as flamboyant as her green leggings and knit purple shirt. Bracelets chimed and jingled as she waved eagerly.

"Hello! Hello everyone. It's sooooo great to see y'all. I just can't wait to get a taste of this famous Okanagan cider I keep hearin' so much about."

"Hi, Sue." Their mom smiled, but did not try to match her sister-in law's energy. "It's good to see you too. Come on in and we'll get you something to drink."

"Yeah, let's let the men worry about setting things up for once," said Sue before she yelled over her shoulder, "Boys! Get your scrawny butts outta the car and come help your father set up the tent!"

Jordan and Todd had not moved from the back seat of the station wagon. Their matching scowls suggested they were not enjoying their trip so far. It occurred to Robyn that the term "tent" might have had something to do with their moods. She felt bad for them, but worried that her dad might offer up her bed or Janeen's. She didn't feel like volunteering.

Grudgingly, the boys pulled a large nylon cylinder from the back hatch and followed their father around to the backyard. Their mother took

Aunt Sue into the kitchen to visit and dragged Robyn and Janeen in with her, probably for protection.

"I swear, Valerie, if I didn't light a fire under those two, they'd melt right into the furniture," said Sue as she flicked her hand dismissively.

"Well, there's definitely no shortage of work to do around here. It certainly keeps the girls busy, doesn't it?" Their mom turned back and smiled at Robyn and Janeen. Neither one of them smiled back.

"Keeps them out of trouble," she concluded.

They all sat down at the kitchen table, except their mom, who made two cups of coffee and placed one in front of Aunt Sue, keeping one for herself.

"I bet you're a big help around here, Robyn, now that you're all grown up," said Aunt Sue, sipping from her cup.

"Well, I try. There's a lot to keep up with, including school work," Robyn said politely.

"What about a boyfriend? Isn't it about time for one of those?" her aunt teased. "Even your little sister is dating," she added, winking at Janeen.

"Not for much longer if Caleb keeps acting like a jerk," said Janeen, although nobody seemed to be listening.

Robyn glowered back at her aunt. She thought about saying something like: *Yeah, sorry Auntie Sue — still childless and unwed, but there might be hope before I graduate HIGH SCHOOL!* She reconsidered and said, "I guess I just haven't met the right guy. Have to focus on school if I want a career. I still really want to be an architect."

Her mom stirred her drink, looking out the window. "I just don't want you to be disappointed if all those school plans don't work out. University costs a lot of money. You'll need a student loan and that could take forever to pay back. We just don't want you to get burdened with that kind of thing while you're still so young," she said gravely.

"Darlin', why don't you just marry yourself an architect if you're so interested in that stuff?" Sue chimed in with an equally serious look.

Robyn ignored the question, remembering the youth employment centre she'd seen from the window at the now infamous Dangerous Designs. It was one more place where she could use a computer. "Well, speaking of school, I've got homework. I'm going down to that new youth centre to use the computers."

"Wait until after dinner. You can't study if your stomach's growling," said her mom, pulling a slab of ground meat out of the freezer.

Janeen sliced tomatoes as Robyn chopped onions. Their mother and Sue sat at the kitchen table, talking about Grand Forks and which neighbour's life had turned out worse as they mixed and shaped lumpy hamburger patties for the barbecue. Robyn listened to the stories with an even mix of homesickness and relief.

"We should have the whole family out here —
we should throw a party! Wouldn't that be fun!"
Sue exclaimed.

"Yes ... that would be fun," Robyn's mom
replied. "The only thing is that we have a lot of
work to do. It might not be the best time for a get-
together."

"Unless we can get them all to pick apples,"
Robyn added in a rhetorical tone.

"Hmmm, I doubt we could get them to do that,"
said Sue, frowning obliviously.

***

Both art and CADD classes were uneventful and
made the next day drag on and on. Riding the bus
home, the idea that architecture might not be for
her gained strength. If one slow day could leave
her so bored and confused, how would she handle
the actual work? Robyn cycled through worries
about her career and irritation at having a crowded
house until the bus stopped at the bottom of her
hill. She could already hear muffled classic rock
bellowing from her yard, getting louder as she
walked up the drive.

"Look who's home!" Her dad's rosy face had
seen more beer than sun in the last few hours and
a lot of new faces were milling around the house,
circulating from the porch to the backyard.

"Hey, kiddo, you're just about to miss out on
dinner if you don't get back there and fix a dog,"

said Uncle Ted, gesturing with his own gooey bun.

Robyn's chest tightened as she walked around back searching for a vacant chair until she came full circle empty-handed. She looked around at the faces in her yard; some were familiar. It was like watching old faded photos come to life, features slightly aged. Other faces were totally new; most of them too young to have been around the last time their parents had seen Robyn's parents. She quickly noticed the guests were all from her dad's side of the family. She'd have preferred her mom's family instead.

Worse than the crowd was the collection of tents. Armed with her paper plate and hot dog, she went looking for an explanation. Her mother was talking to her dad's youngest brother Nate on the front porch.

"What you've got to do to pick up your productivity here is ..."

"Mom, where did all these people come from?" Robyn asked, ignoring Uncle Nate.

"Sweetie, don't interrupt. Nate, you remember our oldest, Robyn," said her mom.

"Sure, how could I forget such a pretty face?" He had the same rosy hue as her dad. She suppressed the urge to roll her eyes.

"Sorry, I didn't mean to cut you off Uncle Nate. It's just that I'm surprised to see so many people here," said Robyn.

"I guess your aunt Sue invited a few relatives after all and they spread the word," said her mom, copying Aunt Sue's dismissive hand gesture.

"Mom! You're so spineless!" Robyn hissed. "What about finishing the harvest? Do you even care?"

Her mom gave Robyn a stern look. "Well, I guess we'll just have to do what we can. These people are family, not strangers off the street," she snapped. "Sometimes we have to make sacrifices for family. That doesn't make us *spineless*. That makes us family."

Robyn didn't agree. She understood the importance of making sacrifices, but she didn't want to be a martyr, either. The last thing she wanted to do was to turn into her mother.

Chapter 5

Halloween had become more about costumes, and less about candy over the last few years. Robyn, Hanna, and Becca had started making their own outfits since the only interesting characters they could afford came in children's sizes. Sitting in Hanna's cozy media room, the girls started plotting as Hanna surfed through a satellite program guide.

"I've got a totally perfect costume idea. So if there's no party, we are *so* trick-or-treating," said Becca, who was always the first to get things started.

Robyn knew they were too old for trick-or-treating. Still, without a party to go to, the alternative was to stay at home. "Don't you think we should give it up this year? Besides, I'm sure we'll find something to do that doesn't involve embarrassing ourselves in public," said Robyn.

"I don't know ... I'm with Becca. If we've got crazy enough costumes, nobody will know who we are anyway," Hanna said brightly.

"We should do the costumes tonight then. Do you still have your Tickle Trunk?" Becca lurched forward and grinned at Hanna.

Up in the living room, with soundtrack courtesy of Hanna's collection of mix CDs, the girls covered the floor in fabric, beads, confetti, paint, thread and makeup to spawn a queen of hearts sandwich board, an undead peasant and a dark punk princess.

Hanna found an unopened kit of a plastic gold crown and plush heart wand to accent her hand-drawn cardboard cards. Becca's costume needed less work since she intended to rely heavily on destroying some of Hanna's cast-offs and darkening her eyes with her brother's camouflage face paint. Robyn modified a well-worn pink and black taffeta dress with skull and bat confetti glued all over it.

Hanna put on her costume as soon as she finished and started twirling around, swaying across an imagined ballroom, crying "Off with her head!" and "*All* ways are *my* ways!"

Becca turned up the music and joined the twirling until the two collided face first. The girls laughed until their stomachs hurt and tears streamed down their faces. Robyn paused, trying to imprint the moment on her mind, wondering how much more fun she had left before she had to grow up permanently.

By the end of their whirlwind design session, only a few pieces were missing. Becca needed a pair of old battered shoes and Hanna was set on finding heart-shaped hair clips. Robyn was happy when she realized there was a solution for both in her own closet.

They cleaned up and hung their masterworks in the downstairs spare bedroom to wait for the next night. Then they piled into Hanna's car to head home, dropping Robyn first. Becca and Hanna followed Robyn inside to look for those last few costume touches.

The first floor of the house was dark except for the blue glow of the living-room television. Robyn's dad sat slouched in his regular armchair and Robyn hoped he was sleeping so they could quietly slip past.

"Where in the he-ell have you been all night, miss-ssy," he slurred, catching her just at the doorway to the kitchen. Robyn's shoulders clenched.

"I was getting ready for Halloween and — oh yeah, none of your business!" she shouted back.

"Really? You think so? I think you might not be going out at all if you keep up this kinda talk," he barked. He didn't even acknowledge the other two girls in the room.

"After you turned our house into a campground, you'd seriously take my one night of fun away from me?" she said bitterly.

"That's what worries me about you, Robyn. You're the most ungrateful kid I've ever met. All we did was have a big, fun party and you gotta get all uptight," yelled her father.

"We must have looked like hillbillies to the neighbours," Robyn fired back. Hanna and Becca fidgeted and looked at the ground, too uncomfortable to make a break for the kitchen or the front door.

"Never you mind about the neighbours. You need to worry more about what your own people think." The volume in his voice had dropped. Robyn could tell she'd hurt his feelings, but there was no sense in trying to reason with him. If she told him what he wanted to hear, she could at least put a stop to the scene her friends were witnessing.

"Okay, sorry. I didn't mean to be ungrateful. It was lots of fun. Next time I'm out late, I'll make sure I call," she said as authentically as she could. She turned back through the kitchen and plodded upstairs slowly, her bag heavy on her shoulder and her two friends following behind.

After school the next day, Robyn stayed in the cafeteria to finish her homework and wait for Becca and Hanna.

The school always cleared out so quickly that it was never any trouble to find lots of table space for spreading out books. Unlike a coffee shop, nobody would bug her to spend money, making her feel guilty for taking up a seat.

"Hey, bookworm." Becca's sparkling face appeared over her shoulder, decorated with glitter hair spray, shimmer lotion and tinsel-flecked antennae. "No ghoul spirit I see? Get it? *Ghoul* instead of *school*. Ha, ha, I'm hilarious, I know," she congratulated herself with her hand over her heart.

Lots of other kids had worn minor costume accessories during the school day like cat's ears, fake scars, pirate and witch hats, fake blood and teeth. By lunch hour, Robyn wished she had rummaged through the basement for her old devil horns.

"Hanna!" Becca called out from across the room. "You're just in time to take us trick-or-treating," she said and grinned.

"Nice; no attempt to conceal that you're using me as a chauffeur or anything!" Hanna said as she walked over. She smirked, gesturing for them to pack up.

As Hanna drove, they rattled off their last-minute costume improvement plans with excited voices and wild gestures. Robyn enjoyed the fact that Halloween could still give her an escape from reality. The girls were giggling as they pulled into the driveway of Hanna's large suburban home.

Hanna's parents had company coming, so a spread of Halloween-themed goodies greeted them on the dining-room table. Pumpkin cookies, marshmallow ghosts, chocolates wrapped in foil and a cake with icing tombstones gleamed like the cover of a magazine.

Hanna's mother swished through the room in a Cleopatra costume. "Why don't you girls grab a few treats to snack on while you get ready?" The girls filled several plates and went downstairs to find their own homemade costumes.

"Rob, can you do my makeup? I bet you can make even this lame camo goop look professional," said Becca.

"Sure, but I should do my own first," Robyn answered with a mouthful of cookie.

Hanna slathered her face with white paste and applied crimson lips followed by dark grey eye makeup. In all the time Robyn had known her, Hanna's willingness to be the centre of attention never seemed to falter. Her parents complimented their only child any time they could, and consequently, Robyn was worried about Hanna's reaction whenever the real world didn't treat her like a star too.

"Let's get going before people start getting here and my mom decides to make us mascots," said Hanna.

Ten minutes perfecting makeup, and another ten minutes driving across town and they were nearing the end of Okanagan Landing Road. Hanna pulled over on an embankment next to a narrow flight of concrete stairs that stretched all the way up an overgrown hillside. Against the dark night, the steps looked like they reached up into the sky.

"You don't expect us to climb that, do you?" Becca said.

"Well, if we do it now, before we're tired, we'll be able to weave back and forth down the side streets and come back along this road," said Hanna.

Robyn and Becca looked up until their necks bent.

"I guess this is where all the new houses are. You know what they say: big money, big chocolate bars," Becca said, grinning.

Pillowcases in hand, they climbed the stairs until they reached the top, panting and gasping. Above a bare, paved plateau, several tiers of identical bay-windowed homes were strategically fanned out to offer equal views of the valley. Elementary kids were already finished trick-or-treating and most of the tweens were dwindling, leaving the streets sparsely populated. After a few houses, Becca pulled a grocery bag out of her pillowcase.

"Check out the party favours I brought," she said, giddy as she unravelled the plastic and removed an egg carton. Becca tucked the eggs under her arm, then produced a handful of cardboard tubes wrapped in brightly coloured paper.

"Ah, a little do-it-yourself fun." Hanna was mildly amused.

"Eggs, fine, but fireworks?" Robyn asked

taking a step back. "I'm not standing anywhere near you when you set those off."

"How about standing near this!" said Becca as she tossed an egg at the front wall of a house across the street. A light went on and they darted behind a bush.

"Could we maybe get the candy first, while people are still awake? I think we're better off chucking eggs later," said Hanna, pulling Becca by her elbow.

Through the hedge and the rough eye holes in her mask, Robyn saw three boys on the sidewalk across the street. She recognized one of them as Nathan, the hot sandy-haired guy who sat at the back of her art class.

It happened in an instant. No sooner had she followed Hanna back out from behind the bushes than the boy wearing a dark hood broke into a run headed straight for them. Nathan and the guy with a ball cap were on his heels. The hooded figure's head collided with Robyn's face.

"Hey! Get … GET OFF ME YOU DISGUSTING CREEP!" Becca's angry voice pierced the air.

"HELP! SOMEBODY … HELP US!" Hanna's voice — trained to reach the back of a theatre — rang out at top volume. Robyn heard Nathan's voice telling the hooded guy to knock it off and calm down. The boy released them and ran.

"What was that all about? Candy?" cried Hanna.

"Did you see his face? That guy was cooked

out of his tree! Wait, that asshole got my fireworks! I couldn't see what he … Robyn! You're bleeding!" squealed Becca.

Shock set in as Robyn numbly fished a partially used tissue out of her pants pocket under her ridiculous dress. She touched the tissue to her nose and blood soaked it quickly.

"I think we need to go," said Robyn, tense but calm. "We need to get away from here. Let's just get moving."

They rounded the corner at the bottom of a short steep slope and found themselves on a completely empty street. An orange streetlight overhead glowed brightly in the cold silence, punctured by small puffs of breath as they stopped to recover.

Still clutching her one and only rocket, Becca dropped to the frosty grass, letting the damp cold seep into the knees of her ragged wool skirt and through to her sweat pants.

"We should just set it off here. I mean, what if we get jumped again? Let's just light it and watch from that lot across the street," she said, shaking.

"I'm in," said Hanna.

"Sounds fine to me; I can't wait to get rid of it," said Robyn.

Becca plunged the pronged end of the cardboard tube into the ground and fumbled inside her jacket pockets for her matches. She plucked a match out of the book and struck it. The wind blew it out immediately. She lit another and, shielding it, held it to the wick exposed at the bottom. Out again. She swore a string of unintelligible words.

"Give that here. We're going to get caught if we take all night," said Robyn and she took the matches and lit one, as close to the wick as she could. The wind changed or she held it at the wrong angle, she couldn't tell which, and the flame travelled upwards, burning her finger. She dropped the flame and the nearly full book of matches broke its fall, becoming instantly engulfed in a whoosh of fire and igniting the candle's wick with a crackling flash.

"It's going ... run!"

Robyn yanked at Hanna's sleeve as she leaped from the lawn to the sidewalk and across the road. When they got there Becca was already behind the broken wooden fence, gripping the edge with wild excitement. Smoke billowing from under the cardboard tube, the first pink-red shot blasted straight up and collided with the streetlight above in a blinding shower of sparks and flame. The sudden hole in a row of lights was filled in a few seconds by a dazzling blue ball that shot past the hollow, blackened socket and exploded high above in a twinkling bloom. A green burst followed, then another red. The show was impressive for one Roman candle.

"Oh my ..." said Hanna breathlessly.

"We've gotta bail now," Becca whispered. But nobody moved.

"Now!" Her voice hissed an urgent plea. "*Right now* or we're gonna be in deep shit!"

She ran; Robyn and Hanna followed, back past the turn they'd come down, along the landing road back to the car. Hanna shook as she rifled through her messenger bag, frantically searching for keys. She flung her own door open and revved the engine as Robyn and Becca were still getting in. Speeding down the road, they groaned, sighed and gasped in unison, then burst into wild screaming laughter.

"We are so beyond dead for this. Forget partying, forget the park, we've got to go straight home," said Robyn.

"Don't be ridiculous. Nobody saw that," said Becca.

"Those guys saw us with the Roman candle, like ten seconds before," said Robyn.

"The guys who jumped us? What are they gonna say if they do tell?" In her best, deep macho voice, Becca mimicked: "I'd like to report some girls for vandalism. We know it was them because we ripped off their fireworks and tried to steal their candy. But being the dorky losers we are, we just fumbled with their pillowcases and ran away."

Hanna laughed and Robyn smiled, relaxing in her seat. A dull ache in her nose reminded her she was injured and she dabbed again to make sure she was all right.

Chapter 6

It was the day after Halloween and Robyn needed a haircut. She dreaded this day every other month. To save money, her mom had always been the family hairstylist, so Robyn never had a funky, fashionable hairstyle like the other girls.

"Mom, I need you to cut my hair," she said, annoyed at her hair for getting frazzled — again.

"I'm busy today, can it wait until tomorrow?" said her mom, also irritated.

"Why can't I just go to a salon like every other girl within a hundred-mile radius?" said Robyn.

"Have you got any money?" her mom said with raised eyebrows.

"Fine, I'll wait until tomorrow. Can we do it before school?"

"The day after tomorrow. And you'd better get up early," said her mom.

Robyn dropped her bag on the end of her bed and sat cross-legged in front of it. She lifted her books out to find a brochure labelled *Your First Job* poking out of her sketchbook. As she opened and scanned the brochure, she decided it was officially time to start looking for paid work. The centre would be open until five tomorrow, she'd checked, so she had time if she took a city bus after school.

***

A mere moment after she walked through the doors of the employment centre, a blonde lady with wavy set hair and immaculate makeup seemed way too excited to see her.

"Hi! Welcome to Crossroads. I'm Monica! How can I help you?" Monica hadn't been there on her last visit, but Robyn figured she actually did need help this time.

"I'd like to apply for a social insurance number and do up a resumé. You guys do that here, right?" Robin said slowly, trying to defuse the cheerful woman.

"Well, you certainly are in the right place, honey!" said Monica, positively beaming. Her energy jumped again at the prospect of assisting Robyn. "Can I give you a tour of the place, just to get you familiar with everything we have to offer?"

Robyn looked at the clock and said, "Well, I

was really hoping to get things wrapped up today. Is there time to use a computer?"

"Sure, no problem. I'm going to get you started with our book of resumé samples and I'll go track down that social insurance form for you. How's that sound?"

Had this woman mistaken her for a toddler? Robyn sat down cautiously and started flipping through the sample book. She unlocked the binder rings and lifted one out as her new best friend forever came back.

"Can I do one like this?" asked Robyn.

"Good choice, but that's a really niche format. If this is your first resumé — this is your first time, right? We should start off with something general. Where do you plan to apply?" Monica asked, settling into a more serious tone.

"I was going to walk around the mall, and maybe have a look downtown. It has to be somewhere I can walk or bus to. I don't have a car," explained Robyn.

While they sat at one of the computers, Monica did the bulk of the work for her, asking questions and keying the answers — mostly related to orchard work — into a resumé template program. She produced a list of suitable employers and photocopied Robyn's new resumé.

"We'll send off that social insurance application for you. It should take a few weeks, maybe a month and a half at the most."

"Should I bother applying for jobs in the

meantime?" asked Robyn, a little dismayed.

"Sure, I don't think many employers would be concerned as long as you can tell them the application is in progress," Monica assured her.

Robyn left the centre carrying a large manila envelope that Monica given her. She guarded it on the bus home and marched it directly upstairs before a cup of coffee could destroy the whole package.

The next morning Robyn got up early and got the same nondescript haircut she always got from her mother. At least it didn't cost her money, and her hair wouldn't be frizzed out if she got an interview. Tucked between binders in her backpack, Robyn brought the envelope to school the next day. She couldn't wait to show off one of her perfect papers, and after missing Hanna and Becca before the bell, she nudged Ivy, the girl who sat next to her in art. Ivy "oooohed" and immediately suggested that Robyn try a restaurant downtown called the Souvlaki Shack where her older sister worked as the head server.

"Seriously, they're really hard up for hostesses and weekend servers. There's a big huge red 'Help Wanted' sign in the window. You can't miss it," Ivy said proudly. "I'd apply myself if my father wasn't so strict about waiting until I'm eighteen to work. It's totally stupid. I've got a driver's licence, but I'm too young to work?" said Ivy, rolling her eyes.

"I don't think my dad would care whether or

not I got a job as long as I wasn't working during his apple harvest," said Robyn. "Like he knows anything about work," she added under her breath.

Acting on Ivy's advice and stories about how great her sister's job was, Robyn took a resumé to the Souvlaki Shack and was caught off guard when the tired man behind the counter asked if she could come back for an interview the next afternoon. She agreed to be back by four-thirty.

Unexpectedly jumpy the next morning, Robyn's anxiety grew all day. Worries chattered in her head. What if she didn't make a good impression? How would she know what to say? Would they care that she had to spend time on homework? Would they let her balance the job with the orchard? Would her dad? She decided to keep the interview a secret from everyone until she had good news.

Four-fifteen arrived and she was at the restaurant early, stammering at the hostess that she was there for an interview. She sat for what seemed like an hour before the tired man came to greet her.

"Thanks for taking the time to meet with me today," he said in a warm yet professional tone.

"You're welcome, I think. I'm just happy to have an interview," Robyn laughed nervously, already mad at herself for her awkwardness.

"If you'll have a seat here," he said, pointing towards a booth. "I've got a few quick questions I'd like to go through."

Robyn relaxed. Now it sounded like her interview was just a formality.

"So, can you tell me about some of your past work experience?" he asked, looking her directly in the eyes.

"Well, I don't have any just yet, other than working at my parents' orchard. This would be my first real job. But I'm really keen to start working and learn whatever I need to," she said, adding enthusiasm at the end.

"All right." He noted something on his clipboard.

"What is your approach to customer service?"

"Um … ah, well … I don't really have a specific approach to customers. The customer is always right?" she said with too much inflection.

He looked at her over his glasses and wrote something else on his clipboard.

"I'd like to try a brief exercise." He placed his pen on the table between them. "If it was your job to sell me this pen, what would you say? How would you convince me to buy it?"

"Oh, I don't know … I guess I'd tell you about the features of the pen, that it writes with blue ink, has its own plastic lid, made by the …" she turned it around in her hand. "Office Warehouse Corporation," she said shakily. She started to blush. What did selling a pen have to do with serving food?

"So tell me a bit about why you'd like to work here at the Souvlaki Shack," he asked, not looking up as he wrote more notes.

Robyn had no idea why she wanted to work there other than needing money and Ivy's assurance that she could get hired.

"Well, I've heard lots of great things about working here. Like not getting called in on your days off. Great tips on weekends. Sounds like a really great atmosphere," she said.

He looked back at her over the top of his thick-rimmed glasses. She sank in her seat. If she read his face correctly, the interview was not going well.

"Okay, Robyn, I think that pretty much covers it. We'll be in touch if we're able to offer you a position," he said with a small polite smile.

Damage control was useless now, she could tell. She had no idea exactly what had gone wrong. As she walked back to the bus, the most positive thing she could think of was to swing her focus back to school and try again when she'd recovered.

***

"Mom, I'm home." The house was silent. "Mom? Dad?" Still no answer.

Robyn lay down on the couch to sulk. Half a minute later, she picked up her notebook to jot down the list of supplies she needed for her major CADD project: her biggest and best distraction. Her mom would never give her any money for it without seeing a list of expenses and hearing an explanation.

Mr. Frank lived up to his self-declared demanding reputation when he assigned them the construction of a model home and accompanying blueprint worth 60 percent of their final grades. Robyn's blueprint was almost finished electronically; all she really needed to do was print it. The model was the hard part, and she hadn't even started.

"Hey, Sweetie, how was your day?" Robyn's mom was balancing a brown paper bag on her hip as she propped open the front door.

"Totally sucked, how about yours?"

"Fabulous," she said sarcastically. "Price per pound is down again and the Grower's Co-op doesn't seem to care. And it looks like we'll be stuck with too many cider apples again. I told your dad, but did he listen?" She looked down at Robyn and nodded towards the driveway. "I've got more groceries out in the car."

Robyn set her books aside and brought the extra bags into the kitchen.

"So, did you hand out any of those resumés yet?"

"After school I …" her stomach sank. "I made a list of everything I need to pick up to build my model for CADD. I don't think it'll cost much. It's for school and this is one of my most important classes," she said.

"I'm sorry but we haven't got any extra money,

Robyn. It doesn't matter what it's for; you can't get blood from a stone."

"What does that even mean? This is really, really important. I won't ask you for anything again for a long time," Robyn begged.

"How much?" asked her mom, exhausted.

"Fifteen, *maybe* twenty bucks," Robyn said with confidence.

"Okay, I'm going to give you a twenty and I want change. I mean it, Robyn."

"Don't worry, I'll keep the receipt. It'll be the best model in my class." Talking faster, she bounced out of the room, calling back, "Trust me, it'll be worth it!"

Robyn was going to spend her whole weekend building the best model Mr. Frank had ever seen.

Chapter 7

Taking the bus to school always got worse in the winter. It didn't help that the first snow came early carried on wind that cut through Robyn's thin fleece jacket. The chill pushed her hard towards the building the moment she put her foot on the ground. She struggled to balance the oversized box that contained her model and keep it as level as she could as she walked.

The halls were empty. She walked through the spacious east wing and main foyer, down the window-lined hall, a dark courtyard to her left and dimly lit gymnasium to her right. The silence was comforting; there was enough noise happening in her mind already. Was her idea innovative? *Yes, for a student.* Had she given enough attention to all the details? *Yes, with the materials she could afford.* The matt board on Mr. Frank's materials list would have put her well over twenty dollars for that alone, so she'd opted for a cheaper, thicker foam-core board.

Robyn felt confident that she would not be graded based on what she could afford to buy — or not. Besides, she told herself, handmade models were already obsolete. In the future everything would be done with 3D digital images.

She found her art classroom as vacant as the rest of the school and cleared a space for the precious model at the back of the room. She twirled her pen a few times, and then put it down. She pulled a novel out of her bag and tried to read, but couldn't concentrate. Running her hand over her hip, she tried to picture her mutant non-tattoo. It actually helped to think that some things were worse than a less-than-perfect class project. She noticed her leg was bouncing off a support rung of her stool when the bell finally rang.

Mrs. Campbell set up a boring bowl of fruit before handing out burned willow sticks and huge sketch sheets. The rest of the class must have been tired, preserving the quiet with a few mumbles and hushed words. No one asked about the box.

Robyn's fluid, rushed movements captured several angles of the fruit until her sheets were full. She walked up to the front desk. "Mrs. Campbell?" Her voice barely louder than a whisper. "Can I leave early today so I can get my CADD model upstairs before the bell, while the halls are still empty?"

Mrs. Campbell slowly leafed through Robyn's sketches. "Sure dear, that's fine with me. Have you handed in your mixed-media series yet?" she asked at regular volume.

"They're done, but I wanted to hang onto them until it's time to hand them in. In case I want to tweak anything," said Robyn.

"If you hand them in today, I'll be able to have your final grade ready for Monday." She smiled her distinctive grandmotherly grin. "You should be proud of your work this semester. Not many of the other students kept up with their assignments like you did."

Robyn smiled back, retrieved her folder from the wall of thin vertical shelves and handed over a canvas board, a modified photograph and a large piece of watercolour paper. She was curious about her grade and resentful that she couldn't expect a similar mark in her other class.

After turning over her model and blueprint to Mr. Frank, Robyn and the rest of the class spent their last lesson playing with the 3D simulator, which now seemed very basic once they'd all mastered it.

"Mr. Frank?" Robyn asked cautiously as the rest of the class clicked away. "Is there any chance you can give me a bit of feedback on my model?" If he could just give her a sign of encouragement, she might be able to finally relax.

"I don't see the point of doing that. You won't have time to make any changes and talking with me won't influence your grade," he said.

"Sure, okay. I understand. Thanks anyway," she said, her voice dropping off as she walked away.

Nobody wanted to go for coffee after school, but Robyn was too restless to go home. Dirty melted slush obscured the sidewalk, but she started walking anyway. The sky was dark and her jean cuffs were soggy by the time she made it into town.

Robyn skipped the pool hall in favour of Lou's Pizza down the street. Warm, thick air scented with garlic and bread wrapped around her like a warm blanket. She longed to splurge on cheese bread, but the five bucks Hanna had "loaned" her wouldn't go far, so she stuck with tea, and tried to get into her novel. She'd read less than two pages when her peripheral vision caught a large figure sliding into the chair across from her. She marked her page and slowly looked up.

"Can I help you with ..." Before she finished the question, she realized she was looking at Nathan. She'd been carefully ignoring him since Halloween. Was it possible the costumes had been so good he truly didn't know who his friend attacked?

"That depends; what kind of help are you offering?" His eyes smiled mischievously. Her eyes narrowed as she considered confronting him.

"I never got a chance to compliment you on your mixed media pieces," he said.

"Um, thanks, I think," said Robyn, still sizing

him up.

"I'm not trying to bug you, but you looked bored and cold," he nodded towards her sopping leg, "so I thought I'd keep you company until my buddy gets here."

"Well, you don't need to trouble yourself. I've got my book," she said too curtly.

"Oh. Okay," he said, pushing on the tabletop with both palms as he got up. He walked past several tables before he sat down with his back facing her. She lost interest in her book, instead staring at his large corduroy jacket on the other side of the restaurant. Why did she always have to be so rude to people? He clearly had no idea about the Halloween incident. If she could just manage to be a little nicer to the few guys who actually spoke to her, maybe she would eventually find a boyfriend. Not that she wanted to go out with Nathan, exactly. Robyn watched as his friend arrived, then gulped the last of her tea and left.

In art class Friday morning Robyn picked up her report card from Mrs. Campbell. She was pleasantly satisfied with 92 per cent next to a bold "A" above a paragraph of compliments.

Robyn is a bright, dedicated student who thoroughly deserves the highest grade in this class. Her commitment to both timeliness and quality combined with natural talent are the makings of a professional artist. She receives feedback well and participates in class discussions. Robyn has been such a pleasure to teach over the years and I wish her all the best.

Robyn was thrilled and could only hope that a similar paper waited for her in Mr. Frank's class. Underneath a glaring "B" and 79 per cent, her second report card did not sing her praises.

Robyn is certainly my most driven student. Her passion for a career in design and architecture is unparalleled and I have no doubt she will succeed if she chooses to pursue this career. However, as one of my most enthusiastic students, I expected a higher quality of work in her term project. Her decision to ignore the materials instructions for her model is reflected in her final mark.

Now Robyn knew what it felt like to be sucker-punched in the gut. The words, "however" and "ignore" vibrated on the page. She slipped out of the room while he continued handing out papers. Without looking up she wove through crowds to the math classroom next to the upper mezzanine. She slumped in her seat, straining to hear the lecture, unable to focus on the formulas in her book as she swallowed repeatedly and bit her quivering lip.

By the time school was over and she was on her way to meet Becca at Hanna's choir practice, she had decided not to talk about it with them. If she said anything it might lead to tears and she was stronger than that. Neither of them would understand how betrayed she felt and how huge a deal the grade really was.

"Hey, you're late," Becca said, annoyed to be

kept waiting. "No problem though, they're still rehearsing."

"It's not like I had anywhere important to be," said Robyn, staring at the ground.

"What's the matter?" asked Becca, unconcerned.

"It's my CADD grade. I should have found a way to do better with that model. I poured everything I could think of into that class and I got a 'B'. B for Boring. Banal. Babyish. And now I've got a dry-as-dirt semester of History and Math. What's the point? I mean, if I can't even get an 'A' in basic high school CADD, I sure don't have a future as an architect. And if I'm not going to be an architect, I don't know what I'm going to school for."

"Holy cow, girl, you have just *got* to chill out. My parents would be thrilled if I came home with a 'B' What did you get in art? An 'A,' right? So that's an 'A' and a 'B.' You could do a ton worse," said Becca.

"My parents don't give a crap about my grades or my career. They'd be happy if I bought a trailer down the road and picked apples for the rest of my life," Robyn said angrily.

"Listen, I'm sure you can still be an architect if you want to. I bet it was still a good report card." She tugged the paper out of the stack Robyn clutched against her chest. "Rob … this is a *great* report card. He even says you'll succeed in architecture. It's spelled out here … what more do you want?"

"The 'A' I worked for," Robyn snapped bitterly.

"Tell you what; we'll stop at my house on the way to Hanna's and I'll pick up some supplies for my top secret special Jell-O recipe," said Becca, cheering at the naughtiness brewing in her head.

"I don't think dessert is going to cut it today," said Robyn.

Becca's mouth twisted wryly. "Trust me, my Jell-O will make you forget all about stupid CADD."

"What's in it, booze? That's not going to fix my grades," Robyn said resentfully.

"But it'll cheer you up, and trust me, that needs to happen. If you get any more bummed about this, I think I'm gonna lose it," said Becca as rehearsal ended and Hanna's fellow actors started dispersing through the room. It was time to go home.

After picking up Becca's "supplies" they sat around the island counter in Hanna's kitchen. Her parents were gone for the weekend, so while Becca combined bright blue powder, boiling water and vodka, the girls gossiped freely.

"Did I tell you I had a run-in with one of those jerks from Halloween? The blonde guy from my art class, Nathan," said Robyn.

"No — what did you do?" Becca joined in.

"Nothing really. I think he was flirting with me. I don't think he knew it was me — or any of us."

"Why didn't you kick him where it counts?

Those bastards deserve to have their toenails pulled out with hot rusty pliers!" blurted Becca.

"That's charming. I've got a mental picture now and I think it's going to give me nightmares," said Robyn.

Becca finished pouring her syrupy concoction into plastic cups and tucked the tray in the fridge while Hanna channel-surfed on the kitchen television.

"I'm sorry, chickie, but I've got to take Becca's side here," Hanna said, stopping on the music channel. "You should have at least told him off. It was probably no use calling the cops, but you've got to stand up for yourself — if not for your nearest and dearest best girlfriends."

"She's just tripping 'cause some guy was hitting on her. Crush much?" said Becca in a mocking tone.

Robyn frowned at both of them. Not wanting revenge was a good thing, she thought, and they knew Nathan wasn't really the bad guy.

When the Jell-O had cooled, Hanna took out the tray and placed it on the table. "Grab a cup and get started," said Hanna. In no time a handful of cups on the end of the tray were empty except for wiggly blue crumbs. The Jell-O soon sent waves of heat through Robyn's body.

"Let's take this downstairs where we've got surround sound!" roared Hanna.

"Bring the rest of the Jell-O!" Becca punched the air above her with both fists.

"There isn't much left, you lush, you ate it all," Hanna stumbled slightly.

"Never mind then. Bring the candy!" said Becca, pointing at Robyn.

Louder music on the stereo had them all dancing again. Hanna had dance training and Becca was a natural rocker, but Robyn was more awkward. Her version of rocking out was a combination of jumping and swinging her arms. Normally, she held back knowing she looked like a crazy bird, but the blue goo in her bloodstream released her to bounce around singing along to the music.

None of them heard the front door open. They didn't see the two people at the edge of the dimly lit room until silence fell and they looked over to see Hanna's father, lips pursed, remote in hand.

The sound stopped and Robyn bounced once more, then jarred by the shock of stopping, she flung an arm over the end table next to her. A split second before the tinkling crash. She realized with utter horror that she had knocked a large vase onto the slate floor below.

"Oh my God, I'm so sorry! I'm so, so, sorry! I didn't mean to," Robyn stammered uselessly.

"Hanna, you're grounded for a month. No television, no Internet and no car." Her father got angrier and his voice got louder with every word.

Hanna's usually upbeat mother glared at them, arms crossed. "And you girls, I'm driving you home right now. Obviously my daughter is in no condition to."

They collected their things, mumbling as few words to each other as possible. Robyn's heart thumped as she tried to think of a way to defend herself. She expected a lecture or angry accusations on the ride home, but no one said a word. Mercifully, they dropped her off first.

Chapter 8

Robyn found Hanna and Becca at a corner table of the cafeteria after History on Monday. Knowing their parents were probably still angry, she hadn't called either of them over the weekend.

"Hey guys, how did the rest of your weekend go? Not too brutal I hope," said Robyn in a tone aimed for positive, but not cheerful.

Neither of them looked at her. Becca continued talking to Hanna. "So I think we can still get our Christmas shopping in after your grounding is over. December eighteenth is the last day of class before the break and you'll finally be free the Saturday after."

"Yeah, we could hit the mall, then go downtown. Sounds great to me," said Hanna, sounding tenser as she spoke.

"Do you guys mind if I tag along? I love the

mall at Christmastime," said Robyn as her stomach sank with guilt and fear.

Hanna jerked to face Robyn and snapped, "Are you even sorry for what happened?"

"Of course I am! I said I was sorry over and over."

"Look, I probably would have gotten grounded anyway, but they got seriously pissed about that vase. It was a gift or something," said Hanna.

"And we were all there because you needed to snap out of your crazy obsession with perfect grades to go to a perfect college," Becca added.

"University," Robyn corrected her quietly. She was feeling ganged up on.

"You know what I mean," said Becca.

"That Jell-O was *your* idea!" said Robyn.

"This isn't helping anything. I'm not mad; let's just take a break and get over this," said Hanna as she got up to leave. Becca scooped up her books and followed.

Robyn stayed at the table, staring out the window in disbelief until hurt and anger set in. Then she marched, head down, through the east hall, past Ivy and Laurie, past a group of basketball jocks, out the side door to the lawn and the soccer field beyond. Slamming her feet into the ground with each step felt good. Rage coursed through her despite the water seeping into her shoes from the slush in the grass. She couldn't just keep going like she wanted to. Skipping class was too drastic and her feet already ached from cold.

Math class dragged on and on as she fidgeted at her desk, stewing. How could her friends — who were supposed to be on her side — bail on her when she needed them? It seemed obvious to Robyn that the whole thing was really Becca's fault.

For the rest of the week, Robyn spent less time out at the picnic table and more time in the library, using the cold as an excuse, talking to Hanna and Becca only briefly at breaks. Neither of them seemed to be making an effort to make up and it depressed Robyn more each day.

By Friday, her mom finally asked, "What's been up with you the last few days? You're lying around the house like a lump. How come you're not out with Hanna and Becca?"

"She's studying for university already," said Janeen, sitting up in their dad's ratty armchair.

"They're not exactly my biggest fans right now. Remember when Hanna's mom dropped me off last week?" asked Robyn.

"Sure," said her mom cautiously.

"You didn't think it was odd, her mom dropping me off?"

"Honestly, Sweetie, I didn't really think about it," she said as she folded her hands in her lap.

"We got into trouble with Hanna's parents. We had the music pretty loud, made a mess and accidentally broke a vase. Now Hanna's grounded and she's mad about it even though she said she's not," said Robyn. She was careful to leave out the part about the Jell-O shots.

"You rebel! Wow, you really are turning out to be a wild one. I'm impressed," said Janeen as a smirk spread across her face.

Robyn glared fiercely at her sister, willing the tattoo secret to stay buried.

"It's not your fault she got grounded," her mom said.

"No, it *wasn't* my fault. I guess we were all to blame, but I think they overreacted," said Robyn.

Her mom put her hand on her daughter's shoulder. "I was going to go through a few old photo albums tonight, thinking I'd find something to frame as a Christmas present for Aunt Trish," she said. "Would you like to help?"

Robyn smiled and nodded as Janeen turned her attention back to the television. It was a small gesture, but she knew her mom was trying to take her mind off the hurt. They had to rummage through an assortment of old boxes in the basement before they found the collection of shoeboxes containing their photographic family history and hauled them back to the living room.

"Who is this?" asked Robyn, wielding a dog-eared Polaroid of a mousy woman with flat, feathered hair, very short shorts and two small children.

"That's Trish, if you can believe it. That's

Kaylee and Evan too." Robyn's mom leaned over for a closer look. "You used to love visiting with your cousins, especially Kaylee. I wish we'd seen more of them; Kaylee would have been like a big sister for you," she said, looking lovingly at the picture.

"Now this one is much better," Robyn grinned sarcastically. She lifted a small square photo with rounded edges. "This lady has totally got it goin' on." The woman in the photo had a beehive hairstyle and thick-rimmed glasses.

"That's your grandma," said her mom as she gently took the photo from Robyn. "I think that picture was taken just after they bought this orchard. See the trees in the background? She was probably standing in the backyard."

"Why didn't we come back here more often, for visits, before she passed away? I don't really have many memories of Grandma," said Robyn.

"Your dad didn't get along with my parents very well. I think he took it very hard that they didn't want me to marry him. He'd never admit it, but it really hurt his feelings," she said in a very matter-of-fact tone, lifting her cigarette to inhale.

Robyn picked up another photo. She recognized the young man presenting the lake behind him as though it were a prize. "Did Dad ever want to move away? What did he want to be when he grew up?"

"I don't think your dad ever had a set plan for what he wanted to do with his life. He wanted to be different though, not just wear a suit and plod off to work in a tie."

"Shame he didn't try out a suit job at least once," said Robyn.

Her mother snapped another photo down on the table, twisted her cigarette into the bottom of the ashtray, and began packing the rest back into their boxes. "Why don't we do a little Christmas shopping tomorrow?"

"I'd really like that," said Robyn. "What about you, Jan?"

"I'm going to hang out at Caleb's. His parents are away on some business trip, so he's having people over," she said.

Robyn opened her mouth, ready to say something, but she remembered the tattoo again and let it go.

***

The Apple Valley Shopping Centre was the largest mall in town, shaped like a stretched "H" with a department store on the north end of the middle wing. Although they hardly ever browsed in the department store, they always toured the dollar store next door. Robyn noticed a laminated poster over the register that read: "*NOW HIRING*" in bold red letters and underneath, "*Extra help wanted for shift work during the Christmas season. Ask for Deb.*" Feeling strangely bold, Robyn checked her bag to see if she still had her manila envelope with her and walked up to the counter.

"Excuse me, could I speak to Deb? I just noticed your sign and I'd like to drop off a resumé," she said.

The pudgy pale woman behind the counter continued chewing her gum as she responded. "Yeah, sure, she's in the back." As if she wasn't sure that Robyn was worth the effort, she paused. "I'll go get her for ya."

Deb came out, harried and frowning, took Robyn's resumé briskly, thanked her, and turned on her heel back towards the stock room. Robyn hadn't expected to be offered another interview on the spot, but she wondered why the woman wasn't more interested in finding staff she clearly needed. Fortunately Robyn's mom was still in nurturing mode and, still unaware of the first botched interview, she told Robyn there would be more jobs if she kept looking.

When the phone rang after dinner the next evening, Robyn had already put the job and the store manager out of her mind.

"Hello," she answered aloofly, hoping it was Hanna. "Yes, I am still interested …" she said to the caller in a much more friendly tone. "I could definitely come in tomorrow." She looked earnestly over at her mother who had already perked up. "On weekdays, I'm in class until around four. Could we make it for five? … No, I totally understand … Seven would be great …

Thank you so much … Bye." She hung up the phone carefully.

"Was that what it sounded like?" Robyn's mom asked excitedly.

"I've got a job interview on Tuesday!" Robyn said excitedly. "I need an outfit! I need to go back to Crossroads!"

The pieces seemed to be falling into place. She could go to the employment centre after school on Monday, then her interview the day after. What she had to do now was pick out her clothes. She would make a great impression this time. Flipping through the hangers in her closet and inspecting the layers in her drawers, she started to worry. Even if she put together a nice interview look, she was afraid she'd have another episode of ridiculous verbal diarrhea like she had had at the restaurant. She slept restlessly, wishing she could leap forward in time until immediately after the interview.

She didn't feel much better walking into Crossroads the next day. Nevertheless she was relieved to see Monica sorting books on the shelf in the still empty centre.

"Hi, I was in here a while back; I did a resumé on one of your computers," said Robyn.

"I remember you! Robyn, isn't it?" said Monica.

"Yeah," she smiled, surprised to be happy that Monica remembered her name. "I've got another interview tomorrow and I was thinking you might have some stuff to help me prepare," said Robyn.

"Another interview! Wow, how did the first one go? Where was it?" Monica gushed.

"It was the Souvlaki Shack, but I'm back here, so not too well. I think I said some pretty stupid things actually," said Robyn.

"Stupid how?"

"I realized afterwards when I was going over it in my mind. I felt so on the spot; I started talking about good tips and not getting called in on my days off. I know that's not a good work ethic; it just came out," she said.

"That's okay. Now you've learned from it. And don't feel bad, nobody gets their first job from their first interview. The way you present yourself is important, but employers don't talk to each other about interviews, so each time is like a fresh start," she said with her usual peppiness.

"The guy asked me to sell him a pen. I didn't know what to do. Is that normal?"

"A pen? I have to say I've never heard of that before. Where's this next interview?" asked Monica.

"The dollar store in the mall tomorrow at seven o'clock. It's for Christmas help," said Robyn.

"Normally, I'd want you to come in for a mock interview and get some practice in. It's a big help. Unfortunately," she looked over her shoulder at a clock, "we're almost closed today. But I can give you these practice questions to go over at home." She handed Robyn a sheet that looked like it had been copied many times.

"Okay, honey, I've got some hard things to say now." Monica sized her up. "Do you live in a house where someone is smoking? And maybe doing a lot of heavy cooking too?"

"Is it that noticeable?" She sniffed her sleeve, flipping through memories of a smoky smell on her clothes, hair, jacket and sometimes her backpack.

"I'm sorry to have to say this, but girl, you smell like deep-fried cigarettes." Monica paused again. "You present yourself very well, but the best advice I can give you now is to take a snappy outfit fresh from the dryer before you go to another interview. Even for handing out resumés. Employers size you up the first time they meet you," she said intently.

Robyn blushed, looked at the ground and nodded. There was more to this interview business than she had thought.

Chapter 9

The mood was much more relaxed when Robyn
arrived back at Dollar Daze. It was too early in the
Christmas shopping season for a Tuesday evening
to be busy. A few quiet customers were browsing
and the store was tidy. A girl with a dark, thin
ponytail was wearing one of the store's aprons and
refilling a greeting card display. She saw Deb
examining a long sheet of paper at one of her tills,
her chestnut hair tied in a large bun.

"Excuse me, Deb? I'm Robyn; I'm here for the
interview," she said.

"Yes, I remember; sorry, I'm just catching up
here. I've got a lot of extra stock in the back office
right now. Would you mind going down to the
food court instead?" asked Deb, reaching beneath
the register for a clipboard.

"Sure, not at all," said Robyn in a nervously

high pitch. She followed the tall thin woman, probably around ten years older than her, in an awkward silence to the open seating area in another wing of the mall.

"All right ... have a seat and we'll get started," said Deb, looking at her papers. Robyn followed her lead and sat down across from her.

"Can you tell me a little bit about yourself and why you'd like to work for ..." Deb stared off, somewhere behind Robyn, then her attention jolted back. "You know what; strike that. I know you're probably just looking for some extra cash. All I'm looking for is an extra body until New Year's — it's not rocket science. Can you work a cash register?" she asked.

"I haven't before, but I know I could learn fast. I'm not looking for extra cash; I'm looking for *some* cash. I know it's not going to pay for university or anything, but I promise I'll be a hard worker, never late, never complaining," said Robyn, energized by Deb's honesty.

"I guess we could get you facing and restocking until you learn the till." Deb wrote in a few spots on her top sheet and set her clipboard aside. "Well, I think we can give you a shot then," she said, extending her hand across the table.

"That's it? I've got the job?" asked Robyn.

"If you shake my hand, you do," Deb said, finally breaking into a smile.

Robyn beamed and energetically pumped her new boss's hand. She wanted to run out into the slushy parking lot and dance, but Deb had some paperwork to give her. Back at the store, Deb looked at the schedule to decide what the best times for training would be, which appeared to be the remainder of the evenings that week. Robyn would start her first real shift on Saturday.

"Thanks again, Deb. I'm so stoked to start this job!" she said.

"Don't worry, that'll wear off in no time," said Deb.

Still beaming, Robyn practically skipped down the hall and rounded the corner into a girl carrying two very large shopping bags.

"Hanna?" Her friend collected her bags which had fallen to the ground, and stood up. "I thought you were grounded," said Robyn, forgetting to be mad at her.

"I was ... but I got out early for good behaviour," Hanna replied awkwardly.

"So you're not still mad at me then?" Robyn asked cautiously.

"I told you I wasn't. I've just been stressed out lately. You haven't been around much anyway. What have you been up to?" she asked.

"Actually," she paused to manage her joy, "I just got a job! I'm a clerk — I think that's what it's called — at the dollar store back there."

"Aw, 'grats! That's so awesome! Now you're going to have money of your own," Hanna said, smiling warmly.

"Um, yeah, that's the plan," said Robyn,

putting her hands in her pockets.

"Hey, then we can go Christmas shopping together!" said Hanna.

"I'm not sure how quickly I'll get paid, but you'll be my first call," said Robyn, straining to hang on to her victorious feeling. How had Hanna managed to remind her of how broke she'd been instead of sticking to the congratulations? It wasn't fair that Hanna didn't have to work for her money and definitely didn't have to save it.

"I'm so excited for you! This is gonna rock! So are you done for the night? Do you want a ride home?" she asked as she shuffled bag handles between her hands.

"If it's not too much trouble," Robyn answered, looking down at her pant cuffs. Her pants were still damp from the trip between the bus stop and the building.

***

Deb was right; working at the dollar store did lose its appeal quickly, along with taking the bus to and from the mall and eating her mom's homemade dinners in the food court. Robyn did learn quickly and kept her promise to pick up all necessary skills in record time. By the weekend and her first real shift, she felt older somehow and more mature.

But a wave of panic gripped her just after nine in the morning as she took her post at one of the two front registers. What if something happened that Deb hadn't trained her for? What if the store got busy and she couldn't keep up? Help — in the form of Abby, the woman she met while dropping off her resumé — wouldn't be arriving until ten.

Abby had been at the store for a few shifts while Robyn trained, as had a few other girls who were not overly friendly. They looked at Robyn and saw a temp; she looked back and saw housewives and future single mothers.

Robyn examined her register, fighting the urge to test it. If she rang a transaction through, she would have to call Deb to void it. She needed more practice, but it was too late for that now. A customer walked in and quickly plucked a phone cord, headphones, and a chocolate bar from the middle aisle. She rang him through without incident and laughed inside her head. What a stupid thing to feel accomplishment over! It was ridiculous to think you could take on the world after a mere $5.45 transaction.

At dinner that night, Robyn was the hero of the day.

"So, tell me, how was my girl's first day at work? Got the swing of things already I bet," said her dad, scooping a hearty portion of mashed potatoes from the serving bowl. He had switched from beer to rum and eggnog early this year.

"It was okay. They trained me, but there's not much to it," she said quickly. "My boss even said when she hired me, 'It's not rocket science' and besides that, I'm just a temp. I'll be back to scrounging for change after New Year's."

"Don't be so hard on yourself. This is your first job and we're proud of you," said her mother. She was rarely optimistic, so it was nice to hear.

"So can you get me a job there too?" asked Janeen.

"How about I try to hang on to my own job longer than a month and then I'll worry about you," said Robyn.

The rest of their conversation over meat loaf revolved around plans to travel to various relatives' homes for Christmas. These kind of plans were discussed every year, but with the exception of the odd day trip, they usually fell through. All Robyn could think of was doing her job well and having a precious good reference afterwards.

***

Both math and history classes loaded on the homework the last day before Christmas break. Robyn started to wonder if she would have any free time over the holidays, so she decided to make the most of her one Friday night off.

"Are you guys going out tonight?" she asked Hanna eagerly. "Is there anything happening?"

"I don't know. There might be a party in Armstrong that's worth going to," said Hanna.

"Anyone I know?" said Robyn.

"No; it's just something a guy in my geography class told me about. Little Rocker here doesn't even know them." Hanna nodded towards Becca a handful of lockers away. Becca was usually the badass of the three, but her recent love of trendy pop-punk fashion kept earning her regular ridicule.

Becca looked up from her phone and slammed her lock into its loop.

"Come on …" Robyn tilted her head and lifted her eyebrows. "I've got the night off and it's the last day of class and I haven't been out in forever …"

"This town sucks. There's nothing to do but go to the same stupid places," Becca complained. "If it's the party I'm thinking of, then I *do* know them. They're Steph Mitchell's friends."

Robyn's ears perked up. Steph hung out with Nathan.

"Yeah, and we barely know her, and Armstrong is too long of a drive to just walk in the door, get bored or feel stupid and leave again. I'm driving; my vote wins," said Hanna. "We'll go downtown for coffee and find something to do from there."

"Sweet!" said Robyn.

"I'll pick you both up after dinner. Rocker-chick, sound good? Phoneless wonder, can you be ready around eight?"

"Stop calling me Rocker!" Becca frowned.

***

83

They found the coffee shop busy, which was normal for Friday and Saturday nights, especially since it was still pretty new in town, with pool tables and a large loft level. Robyn loved crowds; moving through a throng of people made her feel trendy and hidden at the same time. On a mission for a chocolate chunk cookie, she sprang down the spiral staircase from the loft, stopping to let a few kids pass, when she saw tall and handsome Nathan talking to Steph.

His close-cropped dirty blonde hair looked golden under the dimmed yellow lights. When he smiled, he had two dimples, one in each cheek. She had noticed all of this before. Why was he affecting her so strongly now? Because his friend had tackled her? Or because he'd talked to her in a pizzeria? It had to be something more.

She tousled her hair and bit her lip wishing she'd put on more makeup. She wracked her brain standing in line for her cookie, searching for any conceivable reason she might have for talking to either of them. She ran her eyes over the chalkboard menu, too distracted to read it.

"Robyn?" A voice from behind startled her. "How are you? Are you here with Becca?" asked Steph.

"Yeah, we're all upstairs. Becca's talking to some college guy, I think," said Robyn, blushing as she looked up at Nathan.

"This is my friend Nathan," said Steph, gesturing along with the introduction. He put his hand forward. It was warm, but not damp and enveloped hers with a solid grip.

"We know each other from last semester's art class," he said, still holding her hand.

"It's such a small town, isn't it? Just when you think you're meeting someone new, you're not," Steph smiled and shook her head.

Robyn paid for her cookie and lingered awkwardly while Steph ordered.

"Come sit with us upstairs if you want," Robyn said suddenly to Steph, blushed at Nathan again and hurried up the staircase. She watched quietly from behind the railing as another guy, someone who really was a stranger, called Nathan and Steph over to his table. Robyn felt relief when the strange guy put his arm around Steph's waist and pulled her onto his lap. By the time Nathan left with his group, surely headed for the Armstrong party, Hanna was ready to drive Robyn and Becca home.

***

Saturday morning, Robyn found her first pay stub tucked into her apron waiting for her. She tried to contain herself, but after flipping the envelope a few times, she had to open it. Initials and numbers filled the top half of a laser-printed page. At the bottom, next to "Net Pay" $210.57 glowed in bold text. Her mind drifted back to it all day and each time it made her smile. When Robyn got home she was still floating.

"Mom!" she said, halfway through the front door. "I got my first paycheque today!"

"So, you rich yet?" asked Janeen as she continued gathering plates and glasses from the dinner Robyn had missed.

"Well, let's see what the haul was!" Her dad's voice was slightly nervous as he hurried over to read the sheet for himself.

"Nicely done; that's not bad for a first paycheque," he said.

"What your dad means is 'Good job, Sweetie'," her mom.

"Yeah, that's right. Good job, Robyn," he said, patting her shoulder.

After the table was clear, her mom started washing dishes and Janeen went upstairs leaving Robyn curled on the couch and her father lounging in the recliner.

"Hey, you feel like doing a favour for your old man?" asked her dad, looking nervous again.

"*You* want a favour from *me*?" said Robyn.

"I'm a little short on the Christmas fund this year. If I could borrow a little something — just to cover some groceries and the last few things. I can pay you back on the thirtieth," he said.

Robyn twisted to see up over the couch arm and stared at him, her forehead wrinkled, mouth hanging open. On her first payday, he was asking for money; the only money she had ever earned with a real job.

"How much do you need?" she asked, wondering what the money would actually be spent on. Would she be buying her own stocking stuffers or a round of beer for him and his friends?

"Seventy-five. Maybe a hundred, to be safe. Don't worry though; you'll have it back right away. I wouldn't even ask, but we really need a few more things before Christmas," he said.

"Sure, I'll get it for you tomorrow," she said slowly, exhausted and upset.

Riding the city bus to work the next morning, Robyn felt numb. She had worked so hard to earn her money and her dad had no problem taking it. The sky outside was still a dark steel blue as she stared at strings of red, green and yellow-white lights twinkling, twisted around trees, windows and rooftops. As she watched the world sparkle, Robyn resolved to keep her pay stubs in her locker and hide any sign of her bank account from now on.

Chapter 10

Christmas came and went with no surprises. Boxing Day kept Robyn and her coworkers running to keep up with their clearance sale. She was stressed, but also sad that today was one of the last she would work for Deb.

She escaped to the food court for her break and started eating hungrily, worried Abby might appear out of nowhere and send her back early.

"Hey, Robyn," said a tall corduroy jacket standing next to her table. She looked up to see Nathan looking down at her. "Whatcha doin'? Other than polishing off some questionable looking pasta salad. Do they even sell that here?" he said as he sat down.

"No, this particular dish is courtesy of Café Earle — my mom's recipe. And I'm on my lunch break for the next ..." she stopped to look at her watch, "ten or so minutes. So I guess I'm not doing much."

"Well, what are you doing Saturday night?" he asked lightheartedly.

"Um, I don't know … that's New Year's, isn't it?"

"I hope so, otherwise we'll be partying on the wrong night," he said.

"Who's partying?" Robyn's ears perked up at the prospect.

"Let's see … my brother, myself and hopefully a few friends, plus a horde of acquaintances. My aunt and uncle are taking my parents to a ski resort overnight, so we're seizing the opportunity. Do you think you can come? I'd really like it if you did. Bring some friends too if you like," he said warmly.

Nathan's smile was disarming. Robyn had already decided that she definitely didn't care about the Halloween incident. She suddenly became very aware of her bright red apron and boring ponytail.

"Well, I should head back now, but I'm sure I'll be able to make it," she said shyly.

"Don't you want the address?" he asked with a grin.

"Yeah, I guess that would come in handy," she said as he wrote.

She folded the napkin with Nathan's address and tucked it in the front pocket of her apron. For the rest of her shift, she suppressed the urge to check that it was still there. She knew better than to keep putting her hands in her pockets, however innocently, while she stocked shelves.

"Robyn, can you come talk to me at the end of your shift?" Deb asked hurriedly. Nerves tugged at Robyn's chest, worried that maybe she'd been too distracted and was in for a lecture. She found Deb at her desk updating a spreadsheet at the end of the day.

"Have a seat, Miss Earle. I don't know if you're aware of what I wanted to talk to you about today."

"Should I be?" She tried to sound positive instead of panicked.

"What I'm getting at is that we're coming to the end of the holiday rush you were brought on for. That said, Abby wants more weekends and evenings off, and I think you've been working out fairly well. We'd like you to stay on if you're interested," said Deb.

"Wow, yes, of course," said Robyn.

"So I can go ahead and put you on the schedule?"

"Yes, please. Thanks Deb, I really appreciate it." Robyn felt the rush of accomplishment all over again and it lasted for the whole bus ride home.

***

Becca knocked on the front door of Robyn's house as hard as she could through her thick wool mittens. A teal sedan was parked in the dirt driveway behind her.

"Robyn! Somebody come to the door, it's freezing out here!" Becca barked at the curtained living room window.

Robyn opened the door, caught off guard by the unannounced visit.

"I got a car for Christmas! You have to come for a ride!" said Becca, bouncing on the door mat. Robyn grinned, grabbed her coat and ran out into the yard.

"Oh my God. This is amazing. My parents would never, could never, get me a car in a million years. You are so lucky!" said Robyn, rushing past Becca around to the passenger side.

"I know! I've wanted this for so long, and finally, all that kissing ass paid off!" said Becca. She slid behind the steering wheel and gripped it with excitement.

"It's nowhere near as cool as a car, but I had a good day too. Deb asked me to stay on, so I'll have more money coming in. And I got invited to a New Year's party. He said bring friends, if you and Hanna want to come," said Robyn.

"Wait a minute, 'he' invited you? 'He' who?" asked Becca.

"His name is Nathan. He's pretty cute. He said they were having a party and asked if I could come," said Robyn.

"The attacker from your art class? Are you nuts?" Becca frowned.

"It wasn't him that jumped us; it was his friend. Nathan's a good guy. Besides, do we have any other plans?" Robyn said, frustrated. She mellowed and added, "Don't tell anyone, but I kind of like him. A bit."

Becca sighed and laughed as she turned the ignition.

***

New Year's Eve came quickly and Robyn and Hanna found themselves getting ready at Becca's house since she insisted on driving them to the party. Becca wanted to show off both her car as well as her body, ignoring winter on both counts.

"Come on, please, I really want to wear a dress. How often do we get the chance to really dress up in this nothing of a town?" asked Becca. She held out a hanger with a black satin dress covered in glittering specks. Hanna reached into the closet and pulled out a full-length silver frock embossed with butterflies.

"What am I going to wear if you two go dressed like that?" asked Robyn, worried that Nathan wouldn't even see her between these two prom girls.

"I'm sure I've got something," said Becca, digging through her closet. "How about this one?"

Robyn looked at the navy cotton outfit Becca had produced. It was a spaghetti-strap dress sewn over a beige T-shirt so that the one piece looked like two.

"And don't worry; we won't be out in the cold for long. It's just a dash from the car to the house. You guys can warm up with a few drinks when we get there," said Becca.

Nathan's house was easy to find. In an isolated subdivision at the foot of a ski hill, the house, like all the others around it, was only a few years old. Robyn marvelled at the unwavering sameness of each house, designed to blend and fit in with each other like bland building blocks. Why would anyone who could afford to live in this neighbourhood want a plain, boring house that looked just like everyone else's?

Muffled music thumped from inside. Becca knocked on the door while their heels clicked, bodies clenched, hopping on the spot from the cold. Steph's curly head of red hair peeked through the glass in the door.

"Who invited you guys?" she asked with a fake frown after she flung the door open. She sized them up with a quick glance as a bright green martini sloshed perilously in her hand. "Just kidding, come on in," she said and stepped back. A goofy grin warped her pretty face and she quickly bopped off into the house as green liquid slapped to the ground behind her.

"Charming. She handles her booze pretty well," said Becca sarcastically.

"I hope I'm that classy when I'm drunk," said Hanna.

"So Robyn, let's go find lover boy," said Becca with a smirk.

"Just how did you manage to get over the whole Halloween attack, anyway?" asked Hanna.

"Why are you guys both on his case? It wasn't him, remember?" said Robyn.

"Well, you were the one who got hurt, so I guess if you're fine with it, so are we," said Hanna reluctantly.

Becca nodded and laced her elbow around Robyn's. "Come on, we'll make the rounds 'till we find some people," she said.

They found nobody they knew well enough to hang out with after two meandering circuits of the house. No Nathan or any other recognizable face loitered in the growing crowds pooling in the living room, kitchen and hallway. Hanna flopped into an oversized arm chair in the corner of the living room. Disappointed, Robyn sat perched on the arm, watching the hall and the kitchen, hoping that either entrance would produce him at any moment.

"So what does this guy look like? He better be damn cute," said Hanna.

"Well, *I* think he's pretty cute anyway. He's tall, has kind of short-but-messy blonde hair," said Robyn, stopping short as she saw him pass across the hallway in front of them.

"Wait, that's him," said Robyn forcing herself to get up casually. "I'll go say hello and see if anyone else we know is supposed to be coming."

Becca said something, but the music drowned her out as Robyn walked away. Her heart knocked against her ribs as she walked into the kitchen where Nathan stood talking to another boy from their art class. Fortunately, he saved her the agony of having to interrupt them.

"Hey, Robyn, I'm glad you made it! Josh, you remember Robyn?" said Nathan, raising his plastic cup of beer.

Josh nodded and offered her a bottle of pear cider. She smiled, glad that it wasn't apple.

"So Robyn here," Nathan said, putting his arm around her shoulder, "just landed her very first job."

"Yeah, but it's just the dollar store in the mall," she said, looking down. Between the compliment, the contact and the cider, she felt her cheeks flush deeply. Josh changed the subject, but Nathan left his arm on her shoulder.

"What the hell is this?" squeaked Steph, a sour look contorting her features even more. "Why are you hanging all over this piece of white trash?" She looked at Robyn with utter disgust. Robyn gasped and froze, her jaw dropped and her eyebrows arched. It looked like he and Steph had been an item at some point after all.

"Steph, come on, don't get nasty. I think you've had enough tonight. Can I call you a cab?" asked Nathan. "You broke up with me, remember?" he added softly.

"Well if you really want to get involved with a

loser, be my guest," she said, disgusted. She turned to Robyn with an expression of mock concern. "Wait a minute, didn't I just see your father digging through a dumpster, riding a bike with the town's biggest bottle collection?"

Steph paused while Robyn held her breath. "I guess you *do* need his charity," she said gesturing at Nathan with her half-empty bottle.

Steph stumbled out of the room and both guys followed. Robyn ached with embarrassment for a moment, then panicked. She had to get out of there. Around the corner, she saw her jacket, lunged for it and ran out the door, back the way they came and past Becca's car. She kept running until she heard someone yelling behind her.

"Robyn, come back! Don't listen to Steph. She's just jealous," Nathan said as he jogged to catch up. "You can't walk home from here."

She turned around and he was already in front of her.

"Come back inside; I promise you won't have to listen to her anymore. If she's still there when we get back, I'll throw her out," he said intently.

Nobody had ever stood up for Robyn like that. At least, not a good-looking boy. Spending more time with Nathan, since he seemed to like her back, was worth letting Steph glare at her a little longer.

Chapter 11

Normally, Robyn spent her bus rides to work worrying about university or contemplating ways in which her success as an architect might repair her family's life. This particular morning was different. She let herself lapse into a dopey trance, thinking about Nathan and how long she'd known him and wondering if he "liked" her and if so, how much, and then the number 14 bus suddenly pulled into the mall parking lot.

It was Sunday and the mall was deserted, suffering from the usual Christmas hangover. The corridors were dreary in spite of all the glittering silver, white and blue winter-themed decorations. Robyn was excited when Becca came to visit but disappointed that it wasn't Nathan.

"Whatcha up to?" Becca asked playfully.

"Working, of course, but it's unbelievably

boring compared to the Christmas rush. And I can't stop thinking about Nathan," said Robyn, allowing a subtle smile to become a full grin.

"Did you exchange numbers? I'm so happy for you! Now I've just got to get one of those myself," said Becca as she widened her eyes.

"So, mind if I 'look around' a bit?" Becca winked as she made quotation gestures with her fingers.

"Sure, I guess." Robyn's brow flexed in confusion. "Knock yourself out, it's the same stuff we had before; just all neat and tidy now," she said.

Becca wandered up and down the aïsles slowly, stopping to examine and inspect. Robyn instinctively looked up at the store's security mirror and saw her friend slip a package of hair clips into her pocket. She watched as Becca continued browsing, sleekly pocketing a package of tea light candles next. Robyn knew she should walk over and confront her friend, but she couldn't bring herself to do it.

"Busy day, huh?" Robyn jumped to find Abby behind her. "Anything you were supposed to be doing right now?" she said.

"You know, I was supposed to finish doing inventory for the picture frames. If you're on the till, I can get to that right away," said Robyn briskly.

"Go do what you need to," said Abby with narrowed eyes.

Robyn darted off towards the picture-frame section, knowing it would take her past the candles, hoping that Abby had not seen the mirror, praying that she could intercept Becca.

"Bye, Rob!" Becca called from behind her as she walked back into the mall.

Robyn tensed, but said nothing. She picked up her clipboard and proceeded to count and record the frames — until she felt Deb's hand on her shoulder.

"Can I talk to you for a minute in my office?" she asked, her mouth a straight thin line. In the back room Abby was waiting for them, standing next to Deb's desk.

"Robyn, do you have something you want to tell me about this afternoon?" asked Deb.

Robyn stood rigidly, trying to pry her mouth open. No words came.

"Well, Abby here tells me she saw something fairly disturbing," said Deb.

Abby spoke on cue. "I saw her watching her friend pocket some barrettes and a package of candles. When she rushed off claiming she was going to do inventory, I thought she was going to confront her friend. I would have called security myself, but I kept waiting for Robyn to do it. Once I realized she was planning to let the girl go without a word, it was too late," said Abby.

"Is all that true, Robyn?" asked Deb.

"I'm so sorry, Deb. I've never had anything like this happen before. I had no idea Becca was a klepto. I just froze; I didn't know what to do," she said as she searched for understanding in Deb's eyes.

"You were supposed to confront the thief or call security. Otherwise, I have no choice but to assume you were in on the theft. I'm sorry too, Robyn, but this is company policy. I think you'll find most employers would not only let you go, but they'd call the police too," said Deb.

"I'm being fired?"

"I have no choice. I'll need you to leave the premises immediately. I don't think we need to call security, do we?" Deb asked, arms crossed, Abby standing behind her.

Deb's face was cold as she held out her hand beckoning for Robyn's apron. Robyn untied it as she fought hard not to cry. Tears were coming whether she wanted them or not. She clutched her jacket and purse, lifted them off the hooks on the back wall and marched out into the mall, past the food court, past the bus stop and down the street.

The harsh wind of the highway was too much and she ducked into an alley between a gas station and a kid's activity centre. She sat down on the uncomfortable plastic grid of a milk crate and let its cold waffle shape press into her backside.

Laughter from children playing nearby jumped and dropped in volume. Robyn started to cry. At first, a little trickle of hot tears, then sobs took over as she gasped for air. How could they expect her to rat on her friend? Who would actually do that? And how dare Becca put her in that position!

Robyn couldn't think of any excuse for Becca to steal. She decided that she didn't care. Even if Becca apologized, nothing would ever make this better.

Chapter 12

Nathan must have known that Robyn needed his support when he called to invite her for coffee that night. He took her to the Denny's on the other side of town. She didn't see anyone she knew and they sat there talking about nothing and life and school for hours. She wasn't sure if he was officially her boyfriend yet, but he promised to call again when he dropped her off.

Unfortunately, things swung right back to bad when she walked up to the house. Her dad was on the roof banging his hammer over and over. Robyn could see bundles of charcoal-coloured sheets on the porch. She grumbled as she walked past him into the house.

"Mom! MOM! What's with this banging?" she called out as she marched through the living room towards the kitchen. "Is he going to be at this all night?"

"Sorry, Dear, but the roof needs fixing and he's finally getting around to it, so I can't complain," said her mom.

"But at night?" Robyn groaned.

"I know; I'm sure he won't be much longer," she said, pushing clutter to one side on the coffee table.

"Speaking of work, how was your day?" asked her Mom.

"Any dinner left over?" asked Robyn, briskly.

"There's still some spaghetti in the fridge, but you'll want to nuke it. You didn't answer my question."

Robyn flopped onto the recliner, bracing herself for having to break the bad news. "I got fired," she said, looking at the floor. "Becca shoplifted and I didn't rat her out and one of the other girls saw and told my boss," she explained.

"Oh, *Robyn* … how could you *let* that *happen*?" her mother said, drawing her words out as her frown deepened.

"I didn't *let* anything happen. I didn't know she was going to steal. I didn't know that other girl, Abby, was going to go running to Deb. It's not like *I* stole anything," said Robyn.

"But you know that's still wrong, though, don't you, Sweetie?"

"Wrong? Go tell Mister Fix-it up on the roof all about wrong. Besides, it's done. There's nothing I can do to get my job back," she said, finally meeting her mother's stare. "But I haven't ruled out the possibility of suing Becca for lost wages."

"I don't think you can do that, Dear," her mother said.

"Duh, I know that. I'll go get another job sooner or later," she said, thinking suddenly about her plan to save for school — and to keep those savings hidden. How quickly could she get a student loan if she got accepted somewhere? Would she have the money to pay for a move?

"Why don't you go back to the employment centre? They were pretty helpful last time." Her mom was maintaining a soothing tone.

"Really? What do you and Dad know about employment anyway? Does he even care that we always just barely scrape by? Do you?"

"Now that's just spiteful." Her mother's voice dropped and she looked down at the living room's dirty orange shag carpet. "You're better than that. I thought you had more respect for your parents."

Robyn mumbled under her breath as she got up and went upstairs. After a hot bath, she collected her blanket and brought it down to the couch where she planned to watch television before going to bed. The front door thudded shut and a burst of cold air made her curl up tight.

"Hey, Robyn; kiddo, I need a favour," her dad said. "I'm heading into town tomorrow morning and I need to borrow a little money. I'll get it back to you when I give you the Christmas money."

"It looks like you already have the supplies you

need for the roof," said Robyn flatly.

"I still need some tar and I owe a bit of money to a buddy of mine. Look, are you gonna help me out here or not?"

"This isn't how I wanted to tell you, but I lost my job. Becca shoplifted and I didn't do anything," said Robyn.

"Oh, sorry … that's a bummer. You know I'm gettin' that money back to you. And I know you'll find something else. You're too bright to sit on the sidelines for long if you're out there lookin'," he said empathetically. "So, do you have any cash left still?"

"No, I've already spent it all," she lied and swallowed hard. Then a rage surged up suddenly. "But what makes you think I'd give you any? It's my money and I worked for it!" she said as she stormed out of the room.

***

A restless night blended into the next morning as Robyn's anger continued bubbling inside. By lunch, she was still scowling as she poked at another plain processed cheese sandwich, sitting alone in the school cafeteria after a particularly long discussion in English class about an old man trying to catch a large fish in a tiny boat. She felt like the man in the boat, waiting and struggling and waiting, just to fight for something that, even if she managed to catch it, could still be taken away. She looked up to see Hanna waving, already on her way over with a tray balancing a salad, apple crumble and a jar of grapefruit juice.

"How can you eat that garbage? I bet that's not even real cheese," Hanna said with a wrinkled nose.

"It's not like I'm working with a large budget here, getting fired and all," said Robyn.

"Well, now you've got some company at least. You look way serious, sitting there glaring at your food. Why don't you let me buy you one of those mini pizzas? Would that perk you up enough?" asked Hanna.

"Thanks, but I'm okay," said Robyn despondently. Lately every time Hanna offered to buy her something, even something small, it always came with an expectation of deep gratitude, as though she were slowly losing patience with her broke friend.

"I guess I'm just preoccupied with money and school. They go hand in hand unfortunately," said Robyn.

"Oh, that's months away," Hanna said, dismissing the topic with a forkful of salad.

"I know, but I've just got a bit more to worry about than … most people. Hang on …" said Robyn as she leaned over to the bulletin board on the wall and plucked off a sheet of paper. It advertised seasonal staff needed at a farmhouse diner. "This little café is hiring. It would be too good to be true if I got another job, but man could

I use one."

"Yeah, I should totally be out there handing out resumés," said Hanna, though her voice faltered slightly. She looked down at her vegetables and speared a few lettuce leaves and a carrot.

"Of course if Becca hadn't pulled her stunt, I would still be gainfully employed," said Robyn.

"If the job was that important to you, why didn't you stop her? I would have. She was shoplifting and you should have made her face the consequences," said Hanna as Robyn picked apart her sandwich bag in frustration.

After school, Robyn said nothing as she walked gingerly under her dad's work zone, through the clutter of boxes, twine, tools and remaining bundles of shingles. Inside, her mother was lying down on the couch, reading a letter with the Government of Canada logo on it. She was more interested in the paper than trying to shield herself from the noise above, but Robyn had her own homework to worry about. Only a few weeks into the new semester of French and Geography, and she already had enough work to make her stomach hurt. She decided to complete her assignments in the kitchen, knowing the hammering would be too intense in her room.

"Hey, Rob. How come you're doing homework down here?" asked Janeen, breaking her concentration.

"Three guesses," answered Robyn as another round of hammering started up above.

"Oh, sorry, I'll leave you alone," said her sister.

"No, I could use a break. Tell me about what's going on with Caleb," Robyn said, leaning back in her chair. "Is he still on your case about …" she stopped, not sure how to bring up the subject of sex with her little sister.

"He took me out for lunch yesterday, so that was nice," Janeed said, but she wasn't smiling. "I didn't think it was possible, but things between us keep getting more complicated," she said. "And yes, I slept with him. I'm not happy about it and I don't know how to go back to the way it was before, but I really don't need a lecture."

"I know; I'm not going to rip on your choices, I just want you to be careful. You don't want to get stuck in a bad situation," said Robyn.

"Listen, I should let you get back to work," said Janeen, standing up suddenly. When she was gone, Robyn regretted not getting a chance to tell her about Nathan. But then, processing Janeen's situation, she felt stupid and selfish for wanting to gossip.

***

On her first break the next day, Robyn marched directly to the guidance counsellor's office, determined to be cheerful and optimistic. While she waited for someone to help her, Robyn scanned the room and collected every useful brochure and handout she could find. Finally Mrs.

Carter, the youngest counsellor, was free so Robyn asked her for applications to the universities of British Columbia, Calgary, Manitoba and Toronto as well as McGill and Carleton.

"Robyn, I hope you don't mind my saying, but you might want to narrow your choices a little. Most of those schools are very far away. Do you have any family in any of those cities?" asked the counsellor as she passed Robyn a handout with links to online applications at Canadian universities.

Robyn looked back at her with a confused expression. Wasn't it better to apply to more schools, to improve her chances? Unless her chances were so slim that the counsellor thought she was in for a letdown. Did Mrs. Carter see what Steph saw when she looked at Robyn?

"Actually, getting out of the Okanagan is a big priority for me. I think it's important to have a fresh start," she said coolly, flipping randomly through her collection of papers "I'm specifically interested in schools that offer architecture post-graduate degrees," she said.

"Well that's years away then. You could easily transfer into any of these schools after a few years at Okanagan College. You could take any number of routes to becoming an architect," Mrs. Carter said.

Robyn thanked her as another girl she recognized from two grades below walked in crying. Mrs. Carter wasted no time in ushering the girl into her office and closing the door.

On her way out, Robyn grabbed a student loan application package and added it to her pile of brochures and handouts.

Chapter 13

No hammers had fallen on her roof for over a week when the sound smacked Robyn awake Saturday morning. She had not yet poked her foot out from under her covers when something stirred in the corner of the room. She peered up over her quilt and focused on the space next to her dresser. A patch of ceiling was shedding stucco like rain, keeping rhythm with the beat above. She watched, squinting in the dim light, mortified as another bang resulted in a visible crack.

"Mom! Something's wrong with the roof!" Of course there was, she thought groggily; she had to be more specific. "It's coming through my ceiling!" The sky was literally falling as she pulled on her slippers and ran down the stairs. It was faster to go straight to the source. She crammed her knit booties into an old pair of rubber boots and scrambled out onto the back lawn.

"Dad?" Hammers kept banging. "Dad! DAD!"

"What is it?" He came to the edge of the roof.

"There's a hole in my ceiling!" Robyn yelled angrily.

"There's a hole in my ceiling, dear Liza, dear Liza ... there's a hole in my ceiling, dear Liza, a hole ..." The strained sounds of her dad's singing voice grated the air. He laughed to himself.

"I'm dead serious! You're putting a hole in my bedroom ceiling! Stop whatever you're doing!" she pleaded.

"Aaaaaahhh!" he yelped through a crash-snap and the clatter of tools hitting the roof as he appeared to lose his footing without falling.

"What was that?" asked Robyn.

"Relax, it'll be fine. Technically it's *my* ceiling, though," her dad said, now almost a foot shorter.

"Are we switching rooms then?" asked Robyn.

Her dad laughed again while he scraped his way back up onto solid ground. "It'll be fixed before you know it."

Robyn rolled her eyes and stomped back into the house feeling the chill of the March morning air. If she could calm down, she might get back to sleep for a few more hours.

Back in her room, the sounds of destruction she heard outside made complete sense as she looked at the pile of fresh rubble.

She walked over to examine the pile more

closely. It was composed mostly of drywall, wood, dirt, moss, leaves and old shingles. Dust was still filtering the light, but she could see the sky. She turned and brushed some debris off her dresser, picking scraps out of a doll's hair.

Robyn dug through her dresser for something warm and popped up through her hoodie. She slipped on a pair of Hanna's hand-me-down yoga pants.

It was time for a little well-earned coffee and sympathy so she thudded back downstairs and retrieved the cordless phone from the kitchen wall. She called Nathan. No answer. She tried Hanna, whose mother wouldn't wake her up. Becca had stayed at Hanna's so that was no use. Frustrated and feeling very sorry for herself, she consulted a list on the fridge and dialled a number she hadn't thought of in a long time.

She called Auntie Trish and asked for her cousin Kaylee, to see if she were free. Her older cousin offered to buy lunch and tell her stories about college life. So Robyn rushed out the door to make the next bus that would take her to the bistro Kaylee wanted to meet her at.

Waiting at a trendy cast-iron table for two, Robyn stared out the window at the lake watching for her cousin's blue hatchback, thinking and worrying. She wasn't even sure what she wanted to talk to Kaylee about. The roof, her grades, her not-quite boyfriend — none of it made her look especially cool. A small, battered blue car turned into the parking lot and her stomach lurched. Why was she nervous?

Robyn looked down at her napkin, embarrassed that she hadn't bought a coffee yet.

"Hey, Robyn, how are you?" Kaylee beamed, piling her coat and purse into the opposite chair.

"Oh, surviving I guess. It's great to see you though!"

"Good to see you too," Kaylee said with outstretched arms. "Get over here and give me some love, little girl." She hugged her with enthusiasm. "Let me just grab a coffee and we'll start catching up. You want one too?"

It was so nice that Kaylee could smooth over a cash flow issue so easily. Robyn had forgotten how pretty and put-together Kaylee was. Her own plain pants and baggy sweatshirt were noticeably less appealing than Kaylee's stylish, off-the-shoulder sweater and fitted khakis.

"So how is my favourite cousin?" said Kaylee as she put down the mugs and slid into her chair.

"Stressed about applying for school," said Robyn.

"You'll do fine. At least you only have to go through it once. Well, unless you do post-grad." They both sipped their coffees as the silence stretched to an uncomfortable length.

"I want to study architecture," Robyn blurted suddenly.

"Wow, that does mean more school. Do you know where you want to go?"

"I'm applying to a bunch of schools, almost all of them actually, that have an architecture program so I can do one long stretch," she said.

"You make it sound like prison," said Kaylee, smiling behind her oversized latte cup.

"Speaking of prison," said Robyn as she plunged into the re-shingling story. "There's a hole in my bedroom ceiling now. I think that's actually why I called. I guess I wanted a shoulder to cry on. And to bounce some application questions off you. But mostly to rant about Dad's stupid D-I-Y renovation project," said Robyn.

"That really sucks. When did it happen?"

"About ten minutes before I called you," Robyn said as pent-up frustration bubbled inside. "And it's not just the ceiling. I lost my job; a stupid friend shoplifted on my shift. Dad borrowed a ton of money and I don't think I'm going to get much, if any, of it back. I'm beyond freaked out about school and my parents don't even want me to go, let alone to help me through it. I botched my final grade in CADD, so I feel like I've got to get stellar grades for the rest of the year; not that I think I'll get a scholarship, but I'm ready to take a loan. I met a really great guy, but I don't want to dump any more on him than I already have. I know it all sounds boring and lame, but I just can't shake the feeling that I'm alone with this stuff."

Kaylee listened patiently without lifting an eyebrow. She waited, giving her cousin the chance to finish pouring out her problems, and then said, "I think you need some time away. You should come and stay with us for a while. You're on spring break aren't you, starting Monday? I've already had my reading break, but Evan will be on break too. It'll be nice for you to get away. And I don't think anyone should have to sleep under the sky in March."

"Are you sure? Will that be okay with Auntie Trish?"

"I don't see why not. I'm sure when Mom hears you've got a hole in your ceiling, she'll be just fine with having a niece in the guest room," said Kaylee.

They cleared their cups and Kaylee drove them back to the orchard. She waited downstairs catching up with Robyn's mom on the living room couch while she sent Robyn upstairs to pack.

Robyn stuffed her backpack until it was full, wedging her makeup bag in at the end. She started down the stairs just in time to hear Kaylee on her cell phone at a hushed volume. The words "busted a hole" and "she really needs a break" drifted up the stairwell before she rounded the corner into the kitchen.

"All right, everything's good to go." Kaylee slipped her jacket back on as Robyn appeared behind her.

"I'm all packed," said Robyn happily. She realized why Kaylee had stepped into the kitchen before calling home. She walked past her cousin into the living room.

"See you later," said her mother, her glazed eyes on the television. Robyn and Kaylee both hugged her and said goodbye.

"Should we try to catch your dad before we leave?" asked Kaylee.

"Let him hear from Mom. I'm too mad to smile and wave," said Robyn.

Chapter 14

Aunt Trish and Uncle George had a large house in the town of Winfield, fifteen minutes north of Kelowna. The neighbourhood they lived in looked like a European vineyard. Their home, perched on the side of a steep slope, overlooked a long, narrow stretch of lake.

Like Robyn's house, the main building was at the end of a long driveway, set back from the road. The Wells's house, however, had a meticulously landscaped lawn walled in by towering fir trees, and flanked by a greenhouse and gazebo. Kaylee's younger brother Evan swayed a weed whacker along the edge of the driveway and grinned as they passed.

He shut off his tool and jogged up to meet the car. "Hey cous, I hear you're staying with us for a while!" Robyn hardly recognized him. She had seen even less of him over the years despite the fact that they were almost the same age.

"You gotta let me show you the kickin' view from the top of the hill! It's awesome — you can see the lake and the winery down the road. Which I still totally think we should try to sneak some vino from," said Evan.

"I swear Evan, if you get caught doing one more stupid delinquent stunt, Mom is going to shoot you on sight." Kaylee rolled her eyes. "Robyn hasn't even put her bags away," she said.

"Relax princess buzz kill. There's tons of time before dinner." Evan turned to Robyn and said, "Unless you're like Miss Priss here and you need to get," he changed his tone to mock his sister, *"everything put away in its proper place."*

"I don't know … I wouldn't mind seeing this fantastic view."

"Don't put her on the spot like that you little gremlin." Kaylee extended her arm and softened her voice. "I really don't mind taking your bag in. I'll put it on the spare bed for you."

Evan broke into a jog again, calling Robyn to follow him. She was not in great shape, but she caught up to him. He slowed down and started to tell her about the neighbours and his friends in the area, pointing out houses on the hillside. Robyn let him talk uninterrupted as she caught her breath and thought about her own friends and the fact that she had not told them she was going away. It was satisfying to think of Hanna and Becca seeking her out, missing her, wondering what she was doing. She decided she would call them in the morning after all.

"Are you gonna be all right? We can take a minute up here to catch our breath," he said.

"You mean *me* catch *my* breath? It's okay; I know I'm out of shape," said Robyn.

"Well, before we head back down, I just wanted to show you the view of this one really tricked-out place. I hear the guy had it custom built. He won the lottery or something and goes and has this freakin' mini-castle custom designed and built."

"All the houses around here look pretty swanky to me," she said, narrowing her eyes as she detected jealousy in the tone of an already privileged boy.

Evan pointed out another few houses across the lake, including what he knew about their back stories until his stomach growled and he lost interest. Robyn followed her cousin back down the hill, sliding on patches of mud as they went and found the rest of the family on the back patio. The dinner table inside was set and a divine hickory aroma billowed gently out of the vents of a large black barbecue.

"Hi, Robyn!" Auntie Trish waved, holding an empty platter. "How was your day, Sweetie? Kaylee tells me you guys had some roofing trouble today," she said. Robyn watched her aunt smile while she spoke as though every word amused her, just like Kaylee.

"Change 'trouble' to 'disaster' and that's about right. I've got a skylight in my room now. But forget about that, the barbecue smells really, really great," said Robyn.

"I'll take credit for that," said Uncle George raising his oversized spatula.

They ate a simple dinner of seasoned chicken burgers and Thai salad, but Robyn was sure she had not eaten that well in a very long time.

Days of hot breakfasts, video games, coffee shops and mall trips clicked by with Kaylee and Evan, but she still hadn't gotten used to the house. Everything — right down to the art on the walls — was so new and clean. The furniture looked expensive, the floors were heated, and she could tell that every countertop and faucet had been conceived by some sophisticated designer. She hadn't remembered her mom's sister lived this well — better than Hanna's family — although she had to admit it had been a long time since she'd visited.

But she missed Nathan. Even though she'd e-mailed him after dinner the first night, Robyn worried about spending so much time away from him. Would he think she wasn't interested anymore? But it still seemed too soon to invite him out to meet her cousins.

"We're all going downtown tonight!" Evan clomped down the stairs in his oversized skate shoes. A dog tag bounced on his baby blue T-shirt which made his skin look tanned.

"Jason's got tickets to the Silicon Vineyard Modern Rock Festival," he said as he rubbed his hands together. "It's gonna be a sweet show. A couple local bands are opening for illScarlett and Rise Against. I mean, we'll never be a spot on the Warped Tour or anything, but for Kelowna, this is big stuff," he said.

"That sounds like fun, but I can't afford it," said Robyn.

"No worries, the tickets are free. Jason's brother is the manager of one of the local bands and scooped a couple of promotional tickets for us." Evan shrugged his shoulders as though managing a band was a normal occupation.

"Wow that must be so cool to know people in a real band! Nothing like that ever happens in Coldstream. Not to me, anyway," said Robyn. "Are you sure you don't mind me tagging along? I'm okay to stay home if you just want to hang out with your friends."

"Don't be silly; I wouldn't let you watch boring sitcoms while I'm out enjoying the tunes! Wouldn't be too good of a host if I did that," he said, clapping his large hand to her back. "Besides, when do I get to take my long-lost cousin out on the town?"

"I'm not really long lost," she corrected him.

"You will be when I tell the story tonight," said Evan, pulling stuff out of the fridge. He proceeded to make a plate of fully loaded nachos as he talked, trading one container for another again and again. "It sounds cooler than saying that we scooped you out of a reno disaster. They should totally put your house on the home and garden channel with the fix-it rescue guy," he said.

Robyn frowned. "Yeah, we'd need major TV funding to fix that place. Anyway, when's this concert? Is Kaylee coming with us?"

"Nah, she and Jason don't get along. She might be there with some of her girlfriends though," he said.

A few hours later, Evan's friend Jason picked them up and they stopped at another house on the way into the city. The doors at the arena didn't open until eight o'clock, so their plan was to hang out at the second friend's house until then. Robyn sat in a bean bag chair in the corner of the basement, fully expecting to be a wallflower until they left. Evan's friends surprised her. They asked about her school, her friends, her life. Jason compared tattoos with her, and their host, Jon, showed her his collection of trick photos — a wall covered with images of skateboarders, some of which showed him at the Kelowna skate park. She was sorry when it was time to leave, but excited to see her first real concert.

Robyn expected the arena to be crowded. It was busy, but barricades forced everyone into one half of the building, so it looked like a smaller event. The atmosphere changed quickly when the lights went out. A band she didn't recognize took the stage to some weak applause. She wondered if it was the band Jason's brother managed. A core group of fans boldly cheered, squealing and hooting, surrounded by a group of distinctly less excited people. Smoke rose from corners of the stage. Red and blue lights alternated above. The music wasn't her thing, but it was live, loud and like nothing she had ever seen.

Once the headliners took the stage, the building surged with energy. A rush of amazement filled her as she watched live music performed by icons she recognized. Song after song fuelled Robyn as she hollered, sang, jumped, clapped and rocked until her legs ached and her voice cracked.

Waves of smoke came up from the seats below them and she knew right away it was not part of the special effects. She saw dozens of people sprinkled throughout the crowd smoking cigarettes and joints openly. Whichever way she leaned, the clouds still wafted over them and by the end of the night, her eyes felt dry and she moved sluggishly.

"Hey, Robyn, you wanna grab some munchies before we head back?" Evan was still raring to go.

"Can you just pick something out for me? I'm kind of tired; I'd rather just wait outside," said Robyn.

Evan bounced off to a store across the street and Jason waved her over to his car. The cool night air felt good as she walked and as she leaned over the passenger door.

"I had such an awesome time tonight. I'm

really glad you guys brought me," she said.

"For Evan's cousin — any time," he said, with a slightly dopey smile. Robyn wondered if he'd been smoking something too.

As they drove home, Robyn fought to stay awake while her thoughts darted from the trendy skater basement, to her aunt and uncle's palatial home, to the lifestyle of living in a city. Going back to Coldstream was going to be worse than ever now.

Robyn and Evan arrived back at the house after everyone had gone to bed. They went into the kitchen so Evan could make one last snack and found a note from Aunt Trish.

Robyn: A call came from your mother tonight. You need to go home right away due to a family emergency. Kaylee will drive you home first thing in the morning. Love and hugs, Auntie Trish.

Perfect! They couldn't let her have this one week free of drama. *A family emergency? Yeah, right*, she thought. *What could possibly be that important?* Sitting on one of the stainless-steel chairs, Robyn stared out the kitchen window, searching for a reaction she could deliver to her mother that would express how unfair it was to be called back early. Nothing came.

Only five more months and I'll be out, she thought. *Whatever it takes.*

Chapter 15

When Kaylee drove up the gravel path to Robyn's house, Dad's truck was gone and the yard was quiet. Kaylee had plans for the afternoon, so once Robyn assured her she'd be fine, the little blue hatchback pulled a U-turn.

A shriek startled Robyn as she walked up the porch.

"Who the hell are *you* to talk about responsibility? You're such a hypocrite!" Janeen yelled from the kitchen.

"If I hadn't been pregnant with Robyn, I wouldn't have gotten married so young, now would I? Do you seriously want to repeat my mistakes?" her mom's voice hurled back.

"My keeping this baby doesn't mean that I'm going to turn into a loser! And neither will Caleb!" shouted Janeen, very upset.

Robyn was already standing in the kitchen doorway when they noticed her. Both glaring fiercely, her mom and Janeen stood silent, heaving from the fight.

"Well, great, now Robyn knows too!" Janeen blurted and ran past them up the stairs.

"Uh, Mom?" said Robyn, searching for words.

"So, you heard. You're sister's having a baby. Two more years of high school to go, but she's ready for a child now," she said, sitting down at the kitchen table, dropping her forehead into her hands.

"Will you let me talk to her?" Robyn asked.

"Fat lot of good it'll do, but sure, take a crack at her."

Robyn still held her bag as she followed Janeen up the stairs. She found her sister, face down on her bed, crying into a pillow.

"Janeen, can I come in?" asked Robyn, through the door.

"Not if you're just going to lecture me," she said bitterly.

"I just want to talk. Do you want to tell me what happened?" asked Robyn. "How long was I gone?" she laughed nervously.

"I'm eight weeks along and Mom doesn't want me to keep it. I made up my mind after I told Caleb. I knew I should have waited until it was too late to have an abortion before I told Mom," Janeen stammered through flowing tears.

"I kind of thought you and Caleb were, um ..."

Robyn suddenly felt helpless and changed course. "I'd hoped you were being careful. Not to sound like Mom, but don't you want out of this crappy house and this stupid town? Why do you want to … keep it?" asked Robyn, suddenly panicking for her sister, who was still just a kid, really.

"I just do, shouldn't that be enough? I've thought about it and talked it out with Caleb and his parents. After the baby's born, I'm going to go live with them. When we graduate, Caleb and I will get jobs and get a place of our own," said Janeen, in a calm, determined tone.

"Are you sure that will work? How will you finish school? I mean, you're both so young. Jan, you're younger than me, and I'm a mess. If it were me …"

"Well it's not you. I know it's not perfect, but nothing ever is," Janeen said. "That's your problem, Robyn. You keep thinking that everyone should be perfect. Caleb and I are going to try this. That's all we can do."

Robyn stood in stunned silence. Janeen's plan was light years away from perfect — for anyone. She didn't understand what could possess her little sister — her baby sister — to want a baby of her own and give up on everything else.

Robyn didn't know what to do, so she sat down on the bed and hugged her sister. Janeen hugged her back and hung on for a long time before Robyn laid her back down on the bed to let her sleep off the monstrous crying session.

Back in her room, Robyn thought about what she'd planned to say before Janeen cut her off. If she got pregnant, she wouldn't keep it and she'd still leave for school. But can she still leave now, with her little sister needing so much help? It was one thing to decide that she wouldn't be accountable for her parents' mistakes, but she'd always taken a piece of responsibility for Janeen.

Another unpleasant reality hit Robyn. A plinking sound grew louder as she walked to the corner. A cider pail surrounded by a shallow pile of wet clothes had about one quarter full of murky water. Above, only a piece of plywood covered the hole in her ceiling. Behind the wood, a grayish-yellow stain seeped unevenly out into the stucco. That piece of wood was going to be there for a long time. Robyn sighed, and picked up the farmhouse café flyer from the top of her dresser. She still had resumés left.

***

The café was quiet when Robyn walked in and she saw a smiling young girl behind the counter. Of course. The job had already been taken; she'd let the opportunity go for way too long.

"Hi, can I help you? Would you like to hear today's specials?" chirped the bubbly brunette. Robyn couldn't think of another reason to stay.

"I'd like to drop off a resumé if that's okay. I saw an opening advertised at my school. I would have come in sooner, but I was out of town," she rambled nervously.

"Oh, sure! Mom! Dad! Someone's come in about the help-wanted flyer," she said as a man walked out from the kitchen, dusting his hands on his apron.

"Hello," he said with a smile. "I'm Mr. Mason. You're here about the part-time position?"

"Yes, I am," she said and extended her arm. "My name's Robyn. I'm looking for something after school and weekends. Does that work with the hours you have?" she asked, subtly jittering as she shook his dusty hand.

"I think so. What kind of experience do you have?" he asked.

Robyn tensed. She had not fully committed to operating as though the dollar store had never happened. But what was the alternative?

"I don't really have much experience," she said, presenting her resumé to compensate. "But my parents run an orchard and I've been helping out there since I was a kid."

"That's great; good to hear. I don't think there's anything involved that we can't train you for anyway. We haven't had much interest in the position, and I'd like to fill it quickly, but I'll still need to talk things over with my wife," he said.

The whole way home Robyn prayed that she'd get a call soon. This was way too good to be true. If she got the job, she'd have to be vigilant this time. No letting Becca visit or caving to her dad when he put his hand out. When the phone rang later that night, she was thrilled that it was Mrs. Mason — it was even better than a call from Nathan. They arranged for her to start that Saturday.

The job took a little time to learn properly. She had to figure out how to make fresh coffee and clear her own tables and do it all quickly when the place got busy. At least she still remembered how to use the register. In the next few weeks she divided all her energy between the café and her homework. Nathan dropped in every now and again and sat with her during her break. At the orchard, spring blossomed and little white petals covered the rows and rows of trees on their long rectangle of property. Easter brought a long weekend and her dad's plan to start pruning and spraying. The work had been stalled several weeks because he couldn't find former pickers or casual labour to help. Eventually, a few of his friends rolled in and Robyn watched from her window as they unloaded tools in turn. None of them had spraying equipment or the right pruning tools.

"Hey, Burt, you wanna give me a hand with this case?" an older man got out of a truck and croaked at another. The case clinked as it passed between them and she saw the Molson Canadian logo.

"Marty! How you doin', you old bastard!" Another man walked over from an oversized decades-old sedan.

"Can't complain; the wife'd shoot me," he answered and the group chuckled. Robyn looked on as her dad joined the group. He didn't reach for any tools or say anything about getting to work; he sat down in an empty lawnchair next to the open case of beer.

They talked and drank, but no one pruned trees. Robyn could almost feel her mother's anger in the air as she paced loudly back and forth downstairs. After a while she came upstairs and stood beside Robyn, glaring out the window with her for a moment. Then she slapped the wall, hard.

"What's the matter, Mom? Are you mad that they're goofing off?" she said, half-hoping her mom would march outside and straighten them out.

"We got a notice from the government that we owe a lot in back taxes a while ago," she said. "And here he is, getting drunk instead of working."

Robyn took a breath to speak, but Mom continued. "The letter said we had until June thirtieth to pay, but your dad called and got us an extension. We've got until the end of October so we can use money from the harvest."

"We'll be okay, Mom. Something will come along," said Robyn, not believing it for a moment.

"I don't see how anything is going to save us this time," her mom snapped. "When we can't even put gas in the car and my barely teenaged daughter is set on becoming a mother ... I don't know what's going to happen to us, Robyn. Even you're taking off as soon as you can."

Her mom's tendency to slip into depression sometimes expressed itself as anger instead. Robyn didn't know which was worse, but neither was going to help with back taxes.

Dad left soon after that to go on a bottle run on his rusty old mountain bike. When he came back he walked into the living room smelling of body odor, sour milk and some kind of fuel.

"Will, you're ripe! Get into the shower and toss those clothes in the washer," Robyn's mom said, pinching her nose.

"I've been out rounding up money for this family. You're very welcome," said Robyn's dad, exhausted and frustrated.

"I know, but you reek ..."

He ignored her and discarded his shirt and jeans on the floor next to the washing machine. Robyn remembered Steph's jeer about seeing her dad collecting bottles, but blocked the embarrassment. She waited until the last minute to change for her shift at the café, rushing on her way out of the house.

Chapter 16

Shuffling feet and strange hushed voices woke Robyn well after midnight. Her whole body froze and she listened intently. Her door squeaked and the voices were in her room an instant before a flashlight hit her eyes.

"What the hell?" She yanked her covers up over her eyes. "Get that light out of my face!" The intruder switched on her bedroom light. Trent Blake, his younger brother Isaac and Peter Kamath stood in her room, staring at her as she lowered her blanket.

Isaac turned to Peter and said, "Say 'surprise' or something, dumbass."

"Hey, Robyn, we're here to kidnap you," Peter said as though reading from a cue card.

Trent — who failed a primary grade many years ago — stepped out from behind and squirted a plastic water gun at her. The stream hit her nose and splashed up into her eyes.

"You've got to be kidding," she said as she wiped her face, flung her blanket off and, abandoning self-consciousness about her pajamas, leaped to her feet. She had completely forgotten about the traditional grad kidnappings. "Am I really supposed to take off in the middle of the night and go drink in the woods?"

"Get dressed — we're leaving in ten," said Trent, losing patience. The other boys said nothing.

"Sure, but be quiet! Go wait for me downstairs; I need to throw on some proper clothes," said Robyn, suddenly deciding this might be fun.

Adrenaline washed over her as she shook off her sleepiness. It was another rite of passage for grads to abduct each other for unofficially school-sanctioned bush parties. Boys kidnapped girls and vice versa late at night. That the parties sometimes took place on school nights was irrelevant because most teachers were very, very flexible about attendance the next morning. Hangovers weren't exactly encouraged, but they were tolerated. There were even sign-up sheets and keen kids who organized when and where. Robyn grabbed the nearest pair of jeans, a T-shirt and a hoodie.

She waved to her mom, who was awake in the living room, having been alerted by one of the boys well in advance, as she ran out to Trent's already running car.

"Robyn!" A very happy Christina Thomas made room for her in the back seat. Next to her, a girl she barely knew named Olive sat timidly looking out the window.

"They won't tell us where we're going," said Christina, looking excited. Robyn was wondering what she had in common with these two girls for Peter and the Blake brothers. Did they each get to pick a girl, or were they just random names on a list? Better that, she thought, than trying to figure out if any crushes were involved. She was disappointed Nathan hadn't chosen her, renewing her worry that their window to start dating had closed.

"So, you girls ready to party?" Isaac passed each of them a wet can of cheap beer. Christina thanked him and cracked hers open immediately while Olive held hers and said nothing.

"I'm good, actually, thanks. I can wait until we get there," said Robyn as she watched Christina take a drink and looked back at Isaac. "Aren't you worried about getting pulled over? Trent hasn't been drinking, has he?"

"Well no, Mom, he hasn't. You're not going to be this much fun all night, are you?" said Isaac.

"Hey, I know how to party as much as the next kid," she said, and crossed her arms.

"Good. But I'm still not telling you guys where we're going. It's a surprise," said Isaac.

The car pulled into a pseudo parking lot off a remote lakeside road and continued up a narrow drive. The road opened onto an old clear-cut logging site Robyn had been to several times. So much for the suspense. The party had been going on for a while when they joined the edge of the crowd.

"Robbieee babieeee!" An inebriated Becca happened to be nearby and fell into Robyn as she tried to hug her.

"How long have you been here?" asked Robyn.

"Since the very beginning." Becca attempted a serious face, but giggled. "So who kidnapped you? Was it Nathan?"

"No it wasn't Nathan, but keep your voice down — I don't think we need to advertise my loserdom to the entire world," said Robyn. Becca blinked over empty eyes and Robyn knew it was hopeless.

"I came out with Trent, Isaac and Peter," said Robyn. She lifted her warming can of beer, nervously trying to change the subject.

"Well, cheers to our grad class I guess," said Becca as she sloshed her plastic cup of cola. "Rob, I've been meaning to tell you that I'm sorry about stealing and getting you fired," she said suddenly.

Robyn gripped her beer tightly. "You sure waited long enough to say that."

"I'm saying it now," Becca replied with a puckered face.

"After you and Hanna gave me such a hard time about the Jell-O incident, I was kind of surprised that you pulled a stunt like that and then shrugged it off," said Robyn.

"Hey, I'm tryin' to say sorry here and you're just ripping on me," said Becca.

"It's behind us now; let's just forget about it," said Robyn, irritated. "Let's go find Hanna." She took hold of Becca's arm. They wove through the crowd, passing more faces from school than she was accustomed to seeing at a party. Robyn looked around to see that her kidnappers and Christina had disappeared into the mass of soon-to-be Lakeside Secondary graduates. Olive was sitting on a lawn chair next to an equally mousy looking girl and they were engrossed in inaudible conversation.

"I kind of wish that we did something as a group outside school before. We know all these people, but never actually hung out with that many of them," said Robyn.

"That's because they're all snobs!" said Becca, sneering as she raised her voice. She seemed to have already forgotten about her lackluster apology. She giggled again. "How come you're not drinkin'?"

"I've got a beer, remember?" said Robyn as she raised the can for Becca to examine.

"Oh yeah, good! Hey, there's Hanna-banana!"

Robyn rolled her eyes behind Becca's swaying form. Hanna had a clear plastic cup of what looked like white wine in her hand and waved to them over the traffic between them.

"There's my girls!" Hanna's cheeks were rosy,

but she was nowhere near as wasted as Becca.

"Hey, Rob, you'll never guess who's been looking for you," Hanna teased loudly as Robyn cringed. "He's over by the keg back there talking to Peter. Go catch him before he takes off," she insisted.

Robyn found Nathan hovering next to the keg. She still didn't know what to say or how to assess where their friendship was going.

"I heard you were over here draining that keg," said Robyn as she nudged Nathan. She smiled at Peter who looked disappointed.

"Lucky for you, I saved you some," said Nathan, lifting a full plastic cup off the cooler beside him.

Robyn put her own can down and took the cup. Its contents were also flat and warm.

"Peter and Isaac were running late. I've been here waiting for you with this drink forever."

Robyn couldn't help smiling.

"This is a kind of a lame way to do this, but I've been meaning to ask you for a while; do you wanna go out with me? Like, be my girlfriend?" he asked, looking down, watching his toe dig into the dirt.

"Uh, I mean, sure," she said as he reached for her hand.

She stepped forward to face him. He was tall, so she had to bend her neck to look him in the eye. They stood there, eyes locked. She could feel the warmth of his breath. He looked like he wanted to say something. Instead, he leaned forward slowly and kissed her. He touched her softly and when she didn't pull away, he wrapped his arms around her. Robyn kissed back, letting herself melt into his body.

Suddenly Becca howled nearby and they broke apart. Robyn looked up to see Becca, clinging to Hanna's arm, laughing as Hanna mouthed the words, "I'm sorry."

"Great timing, guys!" shouted Robyn. She fought back her frustration and tried to keep her cool in front of Nathan. He smiled broadly.

"It's kind of starting to fizzle out here. I can give you girls a ride home if you want, considering that Becca's had enough already," he said.

***

Robyn woke up with Hanna on the other side of her bed and Becca sprawled out on the floor. Then she remembered. Nathan had dropped them off. He was now officially her boyfriend. Robyn's escape plan was getting more complicated every day. First there was Janeen getting pregnant, and now, what was she going to do about Nathan?

It was a school day, but her mom hadn't woken them. She knew a late start the day after was part of the kidnapping party plan because she waited until just before ten o'clock to knock on the door.

"You've got a letter here, Robyn. It looks

important — it's from the University of Calgary," said Mom.

Robyn jumped out of bed and yanked her door open, instantly alert. "Give it here!" She tore it clumsily as her heart thumped. She scanned frantically for the vital "yes" or "no" details.

"Well, so much for U of C," she said, flicking the page onto the floor after she made it as far as the "We regret to inform you ..."

"Oh, Sweetie, I'm so sorry," said Mom.

"What are you sorry about? You think it's over my head anyway," said Robyn as Hanna looked on uncomfortably and Becca started to stir.

"No, Robyn, that's not what I meant. It's just a lot to take on when we can't help you out," her mother said.

"Can you leave me alone now, please?"

Her mom pursed her lips, but said nothing and shut the door behind her.

"Don't worry; you've got other applications out there. Think positively," said Hanna.

"I'll have to think about growing apples from the looks of it," said Robyn. Suddenly community college didn't look quite so bad.

After a few rounds of pancakes and eggs, her mother drove them to school where they joined the other tired grads roaming aimlessly. Teachers were leisurely walking the halls too, making no effort to herd anyone into classrooms. Robyn noticed Mrs. Campbell looking in her direction.

"Robyn, can I talk to you for a minute?" Mrs.

Campbell waved her over. "Are you staying after school on Friday for the awards ceremony?"

"I hadn't planned on it. Do we have to?" said Robyn.

"Well, *you* have to," she said with a sly grin.

"What do you mean *I* have to?"

"You're getting the gold medal for senior art, so I think you should be there to accept it," said Mrs. Campbell.

"Really? Seriously?" The pitch of her voice was unusually high, so she took a deep breath. "Why did I win — anything even — let alone the gold? I don't think my project was the best. Did I actually get the highest grade?"

"After late penalties on the other students' final projects yours was the only 'A'," said Mrs. Campbell. "You know, sometimes it's the people who get it together who stand out. Your work was conceptually strong, and you were the only student who handed in your project on time. You take your responsibilities and commitments seriously. That's a big part of the real world and I want you to understand how valuable your work ethic is."

Two days later, Robyn sat on the gymnasium bleachers, waiting through a procession of medals, starting with eighth graders all the way up to grads. It had been years since she sat in on one of these afternoons. She had won a few medals in eighth and ninth grades, but nothing after that. She tried not to let it bother her, but she never shook the feeling that her lack of achievement meant her work would never really be the best.

Bronze, silver and gold were announced for every subject. She decided that even if nobody else remembered or cared about this, she'd feel proud of herself. She was glad she had won.

"The gold medal for Senior Level Visual Arts goes to Robyn Earle," said the vice-principal, who was announcing winners for all subjects and grades. Nathan, Hanna and Becca sat next to her clapping and hooting until Robyn was sure her cheeks were crimson. Fortunately, the only thing she really had to do was shake her teacher's hand and stand in a line while the auditorium clapped.

All she could think about was the new letter tucked into the binder she left on her seat. An envelope from Carleton University had been begging to be torn open since the afternoon before.

Chapter 17

Sitting at a picnic table alongside the school's soccer field Hanna and Robyn looked up at a brilliant blue sky and deep green mountains in the distance. Most of the other students were long gone and the field was quiet. Nathan and Becca had insisted on going into town to get a cake to celebrate Robyn's award. It was a cheesy gesture, but thoughtful.

Unfortunately, nothing could distract her from the bittersweet possibility the letter in her binder might hold. Her paycheques from the café were safe in the bank, except for a few meals out, and she had enough to get from British Columbia to Ontario by bus — if she bought her ticket in advance — plus a little spending money until a student loan kicked in. She could save even more over the summer and maybe afford to fly.

"That's a pretty nice shiny medal you got there. Do anything special to get it?" asked Hanna, elbowing Robyn out of her contemplative trance.

"Thanks, I actually do feel special today," Robyn said with a bashful smile. "But there's something else I didn't tell you; I got another letter."

"What school was it? Did you get in?" asked Hanna earnestly.

"I haven't opened it yet," Robyn said as she looked down at the grass. "I just couldn't bring myself to." She rummaged through her bag and fished out the envelope. "It's a really good school, so I'm sure the answer is no," said Robyn.

"Screw that. I'll open it." Hanna tugged it free from Robyn's grip. "You need to know so you can either make plans or move on." She skimmed the page and looked up at Robyn with an open-mouthed elated expression.

"You got in!" Hanna blurted. Robyn yanked the letter back in disbelief and read it herself. It had actually happened. She couldn't concentrate; her mind was moving too quickly and the words punched off the page, hitting her forcefully. She leaned back, breathing, processing. Then Robyn thought about Nathan. *Would he wait for her? Would he visit her? What about Janeen too? She wouldn't see her niece or nephew until* … even just thinking it made Robyn dizzy.

"This is a lot of new information. I think my brain is crashing. I need to think about this. I need to talk to Mom and Dad. I should talk to Nathan," said Robyn, more worried than excited.

"Talk to them tonight, while you're still pumped. Once they see how much you want this, they can't say no. And Nathan's cute, but you can't stay here for him. I'm going to miss you so much!" said Hanna, hugging Robyn's neck.

Robyn knew Hanna was right about Nathan, but she also knew exactly how and why her dad would say no. Her mother might be on her side and that would make things easier.

Nathan and Becca came back with a white and blue cake that said "Congratulations, Robyn!" She let her satisfaction swell into raw excitement as she told them about Carleton. They had a real reason to congratulate her after all.

Back at her house, she invited everyone in. Happy as she was, Robyn strategized for the worst reaction from her mom and dad. She hoped desperately that Janeen wouldn't feel abandoned. It would be hard to feel like she was letting down her parents, but she couldn't stand the idea of hurting Janeen. Maybe if her friends were standing with her; if she had backup and if Janeen was happy for her, this would all go smoothly.

"Mom, I've got some great, great, totally fantastic news!" Robyn said, dancing on the spot, blocking her mother's view of the television.

"We remembered about the awards ceremony, but congratulations again, Sweetie. Let's see it," said Mom.

"No, it's not that. I got into Carleton! I'm going to be an architect!" Robyn waved the letter like a party favour.

"What?" her mom's proud look turned to a frown.

"I got into a great school in Ontario — they have a phenomenal architecture program — and I've saved enough money for the move from working at the café. I'll need a student loan of course, but I can afford to get there." She was in a rush to tell her mom everything, wanting to get it all out before the inevitable objections started. Her excitement faded as she saw the look on her mom's face.

Robyn looked down at her hip, remembering the half-inked tattoo. She thought about the moment outside Nathan's New Year's party, the first time she *should* have kissed him. She pictured the mirror in which she'd seen Becca stealing and the look on Deb's face when she fired her. Failing to act was not an option this time.

"Robyn, I think you might be getting carried away. Ontario is too far. How are you going to make trips back?" asked Mom.

"You've been squirreling money away?" said her dad, appearing in the doorway from the kitchen to the living room. "Your mom told you about our tax problem and you've been hiding money?"

"I've been working, you knew that," said Robyn defensively. Nathan, Hanna and Becca looked at each other nervously as the tension mounted.

"We could use all the help we can get around here right now. How much do you have? If it's enough money to pay off the taxes, I think that's the best thing for this family right now, not some road trip to Ontario," said her dad.

"It's *my* money and it's not a road trip, it's my education. Can you please think about what *I* need for once?" she said, trying to stay calm. She sat on the couch next to her mother as her friends stood still in anticipation. "This is huge for me. And you guys will be able to pay off those taxes this fall. Mom, you said Dad got an extension! I can't give you guys all my money and stay here to rot. This is my chance. Please see that. Please!" she pleaded.

"There's the guilt. *You* need to see that we're in trouble here, now. Taking off to Ontario isn't gonna fly when we need you here," said her dad.

"It's not my fault this place hasn't been successful and it won't be my fault if you lose it. I'm the kid and you're the parent. Can we have a proper conversation for once?" she said, fuming.

"She's right, Dad," said Janeen, standing at the edge of the living room. "Neither of us is trying to mess with this family; we've just got to do our own thing. It was bound to happen sooner or later. Rob, for what it's worth, I'm glad that you got into a good school."

Their father got up, looked back and forth at his

daughters and walked past Janeen, out the back door. Their mother sighed and went after him.

"I'm proud of you sis, you really let them have it," Janeen grinned. "You finally grew a pair."

"I wasn't trying to let them have it. I wish it didn't have to be such a mess," Robyn said as she ran her hand through her hair. She'd stood her ground, but instead of satisfaction, she felt sick.

"I think the mess would be if we both stayed here," said Janeen. "Remember, I'm going to live at Caleb's. I'll be okay."

Robyn smiled at Janeen and walked out the front door. Hanna and Becca sat down and started making small talk with Janeen to break the tension. Nathan followed her into the trees, heading towards the road and away from her parents' voices arguing in the backyard.

"Will you come visit me in Ontario?" she asked as she turned around abruptly.

"Of course, but are you sure it's what you want? I have to say, I'm surprised such good news is causing a fight, but if that's how they feel ..." said Nathan.

"I'm going to university and they can't stop me. It's probably for the best that I'll be out of their reach. Dad can't show up and demand I work for him or borrow more money. I'll be free to just be a student," she said.

"You've got my vote," Nathan said with a smile.

Gazing up through the emerald leaves, bright

with sunlight, Robyn felt at peace with her decision. Janeen would be all right too. Maybe her vision of having a baby and moving in with Caleb's parents wasn't the greatest plan, but it was *her* life. Maybe she and Caleb would break up; maybe they would be a happy family. But that was up to them.

Robyn was reassured by the idea she still had July and August to spend with Nathan and her friends before she had to leave. She'd come back and see them in the summers, and maybe they could come and stay with her. The campus dorms were bound to have computers — she could use e-mail regularly and finally get on Facebook or MySpace. She'd find a way to hang on to what was important.

On the surrounding trees, small green apples had already sprouted in a few places, reminding Robyn that in the grand scheme of things, her life had just begun.